Les Belles Soeurs

LES BELLES SOEURS

MICHEL TREMBLAY

Translated by John Van Burek & Bill Glassco

Talonbooks : Vancouver : 1974

published with assistance from the Canada Council

Talonbooks
201 1019 East Cordova
Vancouver
British Columbia V6A 1M8
Canada

This book was typeset by Beverly Matsu, designed by Gordon Fidler with Jorge Saia and printed in Canada by Webcom for Talonbooks.

The backcover photograph was taken by Barry Philp.

Seventh printing: February 1987
Eighth printing: October 1989

First published by Les Editions Leméac Inc., Montréal, Québec.

Canadian Cataloguing in Publication Data

Tremblay, Michel, 1943—
    [Les belles soeurs. English]
    Les belles soeurs

    Translation of Les belles soeurs.
    A play.
    ISBN 0-888922-081-6 pa.

    I. Title. II. Title: Les belles soeurs.
English.
PS8539.R47B413   C842'.5'4   C75-4179-X
PQ3919.2.T73B413

Les Belles Soeurs was first performed at Théâtre du Rideau-Vert in Montréal, Québec, on August 28, 1968, with the following cast:

Germaine Lauzon	Denise Proulx
Linda Lauzon	Odette Gagnon
Rose Ouimet	Denise Filiathraùlt
Gabrielle Jodoin	Lucille Bélair
Lisette de Courval	Hélène Loiselle
Marie-Ange Brouillette	Marthe Choquette
Yvette Longpré	Sylvie Heppel
Des-Neiges Verrette	Denise de Jaguère
Thérèse Dubuc	Germaine Giroux
Olivine Dubuc	Nicole Leblanc
Angéline Sauvé	Anne-Marie Ducharme
Rhéauna Bibeau	Germaine Lemyre
Ginette Ménard	Josée Beauregard
Pierrette Guérin	Luce Guilbeault

Directed by André Brassard

Les Belles Soeurs was first performed in English at the St. Lawrence Centre in Toronto, Ontario, on April 3, 1973, with the following cast:

Germaine Lauzon	Candy Kane
Linda Lauzon	Elva-May Hoover
Rose Ouimet	Monique Mercure
Gabrielle Jodoin	Araby Lockhart
Lisette de Courval	Mia Anderson
Marie-Ange Brouillette	Deborah Packer
Yvette Longpré	Louise Nichol
Des-Neiges Verrette	Maureen Fitzgerald
Thérèse Dubuc	Irene Hogan
Olivine Dubuc	Lilian Lewis
Angéline Sauvé	Patricia Hamilton
Rhéauna Bibeau	Nancy Kerr
Lise Paquette	Trudy Young
Ginette Ménard	Suzette Couture
Pierrette Guérin	Melanie Morse

Directed by André Brassard

ACT ONE

LINDA LAUZON enters. She sees four boxes in the middle of the kitchen.

LINDA:
> Sweet Jesus, what's that? Ma!

GERMAINE:
> Is that you, Linda?

LINDA:
> Yeah! What are all these boxes doing in the kitchen?

GERMAINE:
> They're my stamps.

LINDA:
> No kidding, already? That was fast.

GERMAINE:
> Yeah, it surprised me too. They came this morning right after you left. I heard the doorbell. I went to answer it and there's this big fellow standing in the hall. Oh, you would have liked him, Linda. Just your

type. About twenty-two, maybe twenty-three. Dark
curly hair. You know, nice little moustache. Really
handsome. Anyway, he says to me, "Are you the
lady of the house, Mme. Germaine Lauzon?" I said,
"That's me all right." And he says, "Good, I've brought
your stamps." Linda, I was so excited. I didn't know
what to say. Next thing I knew, two men were
bringing in the boxes and the other one's giving me
this big speech. What a smoothie. You should've
heard him, Linda. And so good-looking . . . I know
you would have liked him.

LINDA:
Well, come on. What did he say?

GERMAINE:
I can't remember. I was too excited. I think it was
something about the company he works for and how
glad they are I won the stamps . . . That I was very
lucky, you know . . . Me, I didn't know what to
say. I wish your father had been here. He could have
talked to him. I didn't even thank him . . .

LINDA:
A million stamps. Jeez, we'll spend the rest of our
lives just putting them in the books. Four crates of
'em!

GERMAINE:
There's only three with stamps. The other one's
booklets. But look, I had an idea. We'll never be
able to do it alone. You going out tonight?

LINDA:
Yeah, Robert's supposed to call me . . .

GERMAINE:
Why don't you go out tomorrow night? Listen, I had
an idea. I phoned all my sisters, your father's sister

and I've been to see the neighbours and I've invited them all over to paste stamps with us tonight. I'm gonna give a stamp-pasting party. Isn't that a good idea? I bought some peanuts and potato chips and I've sent the kids to get some coke . . .

LINDA:

But Ma, I always go out on Thursday night. You know that. It's our night out. We're gonna go to the show.

GERMAINE:

You can't leave me alone on a night like this. I've got fifteen people coming . . .

LINDA:

Are you out of your mind? Fifteen people in this kitchen? There's no way. And you know we can't use the rest of the house. The painters are here. Jesus, Ma! Sometimes you're really dumb.

GERMAINE:

That's right. You've always said so. I'm dumb. Okay, Linda, go ahead. Do what you like. That's all you ever do anyway. It's nothing new. Christ, I can't have a bit of pleasure for myself. Someone's always got to spoil it for me. It's okay, Linda, if that's what you want. Go ahead. Go to your goddamn show!

LINDA:

Come on, Ma, try to understand.

GERMAINE:

I don't want to understand. I don't even want to hear about it. I kill myself for the whole bunch of you and what do I get in return? Nothing! A big fat nothing! You can't even do me a little favour! I'm warning you, Linda. I'm sick and tired of waiting on you. You and everyone else. I'm not a slave, you know. I've got a million stamps to paste and I'm not

9

about to do it by myself. And what's more, those stamps are for the whole family. Which means everybody's gotta do their share. Look at your poor father. He's on his night shift, but he says he'll help tomorrow if we don't get done tonight. You act like I'm asking for the moon. Why don't you help me for a change instead of wasting your time on that moron?

LINDA:
Robert is not a moron.

GERMAINE:
Boy, I knew you were stupid, but not that stupid. When are you going to realize that your precious Robert is a lazy bum? He doesn't even make sixty bucks a week. All he can do is take you to some two-bit show on Thursday nights. I'm telling you, Linda. Take your mother's advice. Keep hanging around with that dope and you'll end up just like him. You want to marry a shoe-gluer and be a strapper all your life?

LINDA:
Shut up, Ma! You don't know what you're saying. Anyway, forget it . . . I'll stay home . . . Just stop screaming about it, okay? And by the way, Robert's due for a raise pretty soon and he'll be making a lot more. The boss told me himself. He'll be into the big money in no time and they'll make him a small boss. You wait. Eighty bucks a week is nothing to laugh at. Anyway . . . I'm gonna go phone him and tell him I can't go to the show . . . Hey, why don't I tell him to come and glue stamps with us?

GERMAINE:
Mother of God, I just told you I can't stand him and you ask me if you can bring him home tonight. Where the hell are your brains? What did I do to make God in heaven send me such idiots? Just this afternoon, I ask your brother to get me a bag of onions and he comes home with a quart of milk.

It's ridiculous! I have to repeat everything fifty times. No wonder I lose my temper. I told you, Linda. The party's for girls. Just girls. Your Robert's not queer, is he?

LINDA:

Okay, okay! Don't get so excited. I'll tell him not to come. Jesus, you can't do a bloody thing around here. You think I feel like gluing stamps after working all day?

LINDA starts to dial a number.

Why don't you go dust in the living room, eh? You don't have to listen to what I'm going to say . . . "Hello, is Robert there? . . . When do you expect him? . . . Okay, will you tell him that Linda phoned? . . . Fine, Mme. Bergeron. And you? . . . That's good . . . Okay then, thanks a lot. Bye."

She hangs up. The phone rings right away.

"Hello?" . . . Ma, it's for you.

GERMAINE: *entering*

Twenty years old and you still don't know how to answer the phone. When are you gonna learn to say, "One moment, please?"

LINDA:

It's only Aunt Rose. Why should I be polite to her?

GERMAINE: *putting her hand over the receiver*

Will you be quiet! You want her to hear you?

LINDA:

Who gives a shit?

GERMAINE:

"Hello? Oh, it's you, Rose . . . Yeah, they've come . . .
How 'bout that, eh? A million stamps! They're
sitting right here in front of me and I still can't
believe it. A million of them. I don't know how
much that is, but who cares. A million's a million . . .
Sure, they sent a catalogue. I already had last years,
but this one's for this year. So it's a lot better . . .
Besides, the old one was falling apart . . . Wait'll
you see the stuff they got. You won't believe it. I
think I'll be able to take everything and do over the
whole house. I'm gonna get a new stove, new fridge,
new kitchen set. I think I'll take the red one with the
gold stars. I don't think you've seen that one, have
you? . . . Oh, it's nice, Rose. Really nice. I'm gonna
get new pots, new cutlery, a full set of dishes, salt
and pepper shakers . . . Oh, and you know those
glasses with the "caprice" design. Well, I'm taking a
set of those too. Mme. de Courval got a set last
year. She paid a fortune for them, but I'm getting
mine for free. She'll be mad as hell, eh? . . . What?
. . . Yeah, she'll be here tonight. They've got those
chrome tins for flour and sugar and coffee . . . I'm
taking the whole thing. I'm also getting a Colonial
bedroom suite with full accessories. There's curtains,
dresser-covers, one of those things you put on the
floor beside the bed . . . No, dear, not that . . . New
wallpaper . . . Not the floral. Henri can't sleep with
flowers . . . I'm telling you, Rose. It's gonna be one
beautiful bedroom. And the living room. Wait till
you hear this . . . I've got a big TV with a built-in
stereo, a synthetic nylon carpet, real paintings . . .
You know those Chinese paintings I've always wanted,
the ones with the velvet? . . . Aren't they though?
But will you get a load of this . . . I'm gonna have
the same crystal platters as your sister-in-law, Aline!
I'm not sure, but I think mine are even nicer. There's
ashtrays, lamps. Fantastic, eh? I guess that's about it
for the living room . . . There's an electric razor for

Henri to shave with, shower curtains . . . So what?
We'll put one in. It all comes with the stamps.
There's a sunken bathtub, a new sink, bathing suits
for everyone . . . No, Rose, I am not too fat. Don't
be smart. Now listen, I'm gonna re-do the kid's room
completely. Have you seen what they've got for kids'
bedrooms? Rose, it's stunning! They've got Mickey
Mouse all over everything. And for Linda's room . . .
Okay, sure, you can look at it when you get here.
Come over right away though, 'cause the others will
be here any minute. I told them to come early. You
know, it's gonna take forever to paste all those stamps."

MARIE-ANGE BROUILLETTE enters.

"Okay, I've gotta hang up. Mme. Brouillette's just
arrived. Okay, yeah . . . Yeah . . . Bye!"

MARIE-ANGE:
I can't help it, Mme. Lauzon. I'm jealous.

GERMAINE:
Well, I know what you mean. It's quite an event.
Excuse me for a second, Mme. Brouillette. I'm not
quite ready. I was talking to my sister, Rose. We can
see each other across the alley, you know. It's very
handy.

MARIE-ANGE:
Is she gonna be here?

GERMAINE:
You bet! She wouldn't miss this for love or money.
Here, have a seat. You can look at the catalogue
while you're waiting. You won't believe the lovely
things they've got. And I'm taking every one of
them, Mme. Brouillette. The whole catalogue.

GERMAINE goes into her bedroom.

MARIE-ANGE:

You won't catch me winning something like that.
Not in a million years. I live in shit and that's where
I'll be till the day I die. A million stamps! Jesus, a
whole house. If I don't stop thinking about it I'm
gonna go nuts. It's always the way. The ones with
all the luck deserve it the least. What's she ever done,
Mme. Lauzon, to deserve all this? Nothing! Not a
goddamn thing. She's no better looking than me. In
fact, she's no better period. These contests shouldn't
be allowed. The priest the other day was right. They
ought to be abolished. Why should she win a million
stamps and not me? Why? It's not fair. Me too, I got
kids to keep clean and I work as hard as she does
wiping their asses all day long. In fact, my kids are a
lot cleaner than hers. What do you think I'm all skin
and bones for? 'Cause I work like a carthorse. That's
why. But look at her. She's fat as a pig. And now I
gotta live across the hall from her and listen to her
bragging about her brand new home. I tell you, I
can't stand it. Oh, there'll be no end to her smart-
ass comments. She's just the type, the loud-mouthed
bitch. It's all I'll be hearing for the next five years.
"I got this with my stamps, I got that with my
stamps." It's enough to make you puke! Believe
me, I'm not gonna spend my life in this shit while
Madame Fatso here goes swimming in velvet. It's
not fair and I'm sick of it. I'm sick of killing myself
for nothing. My life is nothing. A big fat nothing. I
haven't a cent to my name. I'm sick to death, I tell
you. I'm sick to death of this stupid, rotten life!

*During the monologue, GABRIELLE JODOIN,
ROSE OUIMET, YVETTE LONGPRE and
LISETTE DE COURVAL have entered. They
take their places in the kitchen without
paying attention to MARIE-ANGE. The five
women get up and turn to the audience.*

14

THE FIVE WOMEN: *together*
> This stupid, rotten life! Monday!

LISETTE:
> When the sun with his rays starts caressing the little
> flowers in the fields and the little birds open wide
> their little beaks to send forth their little cries to
> heaven . . .

THE OTHERS:
> I get up to fix breakfast. Toast, coffee, bacon, eggs.
> I nearly go nuts just getting the others out of bed.
> The kids leave for school. My husband goes to work.

MARIE-ANGE:
> Not mine. He's unemployed. He stays in bed.

THE FIVE WOMEN:
> Then I work. I work like a demon. I don't stop till
> noon. I wash . . . Dresses, shirts, stockings, sweaters,
> pants, underpants, bras. The works. I scrub it. I wring
> it out. I scrub it again. I rinse it . . . My hands are
> chapped. My back is sore. I curse like hell. At noon,
> the kids come home. They eat like pigs. They mess
> up the house. They leave. In the afternoon, I hang
> out the wash, the biggest pain of all. When I finish
> with that, I start the supper. They all come home.
> They're tired and ratty. We all fight. But at night we
> watch TV. Tuesday.

LISETTE:
> When the sun with his rays . . .

THE OTHERS:
> I get up to fix breakfast. The same goddamn thing.
> Toast, coffee, bacon, eggs. I get them out of bed
> and kick them out the door. Then it's the ironing. I
> work, I work, I work and I work. It's noon before I

know it and the kids are mad because lunch isn't
ready. I make baloney sandwiches. I work all afternoon. Suppertime comes. We all fight. But at night
we watch TV. Wednesday . . . Shopping day. I walk all
day long. I break my back carrying parcels this big. I
come home beat and I've got to make supper. When
the others get home I look like I'm dead. I am. My
husband bitches. The kids scream. We all fight. But
at night we watch TV. Thursday and Friday . . . Same
thing. I work. I slave. I kill myself for a pack of
morons. Then Saturday, to top it all off, I've got
the kids on my back and we all fight. But at night,
we watch TV. Sunday I take the family, climb on
the bus and go for supper with the mother-in-law.
I watch the kids like a hawk, laugh at the old man's
jokes, eat the old lady's food, which everyone says is
better than mine . . . At night, we watch TV. I'm
sick of this stupid, rotten life! This stupid, rotten
life! This stupid, rotten life. This stup . . .

>   *They sit down suddenly.*

LISETTE:
>   On my last trip to Europe . . .

ROSE:
>   There she goes with her Europe again. Get her going
>   on that and she's good for the whole night.

>   *DES-NEIGES VERRETTE comes in. Discreet
>   little greetings are heard.*

LISETTE:
>   I only wished to say that in Europe they don't have
>   stamps. I mean, they have stamps, but not this kind.
>   Only letter stamping stamps.

DES-NEIGES:
>   No kidding! You mean you don't get presents like
>   you do here? Boy, that Europe sounds like a pretty
>   dull place.

LISETTE:

    Oh no, it's very nice in spite of that . . .

MARIE-ANGE:

    I'm not against stamps, mind you. They're very
    convenient. If it weren't for the stamps, I'd still be
    waiting for that thing to grind my meat with. What
    I don't like is the contests.

LISETTE:

    But why? They can make a whole family happy.

MARIE-ANGE:

    Maybe so. But they're a pain in the ass for the people
    next door.

LISETTE:

    Mme. Brouillette, your language! It doesn't cost
    anything to be polite, you know. Look at me.

MARIE-ANGE:

    I talk the way I talk. And I say what I got to say.
    Anyway, I never went to Europe, so I can't afford to
    talk like you.

ROSE:

    Hey, you two, cut that out! We didn't come here to
    fight. You keep it up, I'm going down those stairs,
    across that alley and home.

GABRIELLE:

    I wonder what's taking Germaine so long. Germaine!

GERMAINE: *from the bedroom*

    Be there in a minute. I'm having a hard time getting
    into my . . . Well, I'm having a hard time . . . Is Linda
    there?

GABRIELLE:

Linda! Linda! No, she's not here.

MARIE-ANGE:

I think I saw her go out a while ago.

GERMAINE:

Don't tell me she's snuck out, the little bitch.

GABRIELLE:

Can we start pasting stamps in the meantime?

GERMAINE:

No wait! I'll show you what to do. Don't start without me. Just chat for a bit.

GABRIELLE:

"Chat for a bit?" What are we going to chat about . . .

The telephone rings.

ROSE:

Oh my God, that scared me! "Hello! No, she's out, but if you want to wait I think she'll be back in a minute."

She puts the receiver down, goes out on the balcony and shouts.

Linda! Linda, telephone!

LISETTE:

Well, Mme. Longpré, how does your daughter Claudette like being married?

YVETTE:

Oh, she likes it just fine. She's having a ball. She told me all about her honeymoon, you know.

GABRIELLE:
Where is it they went to?

YVETTE:
Well, he won a trip to the Canary Islands, eh? So you
you see, they had to put the wedding ahead a bit . . .

ROSE: *laughing*
The Canary Islands! A honeymoon in the bird shit,
eh?

GABRIELLE:
Come on, Rose!

ROSE:
What?

DES-NEIGES:
The Canary Islands, where's that?

LISETTE:
We stopped by there, my husband and I, on our last
trip to Europe. It's a real . . . It's a very nice country.
The women only wear skirts, you know.

ROSE:
My husband would like that!

LISETTE:
But I'm afraid the people there are not very clean.
Of course, in Europe they never wash either.

DES-NEIGES:
It shows too. Look at those Italians next door to me.
You can't imagine how that woman stinks.

They all burst out laughing.

LISETTE: *insinuating*

Did you ever notice her clothesline on Monday afternoon?

DES-NEIGES:

No, why?

LISETTE:

Well, all I know is this . . . Those people never wear any underwear.

MARIE-ANGE:

No kidding!

ROSE:

I don't believe it!

YVETTE:

You gotta be joking!

LISETTE:

It's the God's truth! Take a look for yourselves next Monday. You'll see.

YVETTE:

No wonder they stink.

MARIE-ANGE:

Maybe she's too modest to hang them outside.

The others laugh.

LISETTE:

Too modest! A European? Those people don't know what modesty is! Why look at their movies you see on TV. It's dreadful. They stand right in the middle of the street and kiss. On the mouth too! It's in their blood, you know. You just keep your eye on that Italian's daughter when she brings her friends around . . . Her *boy*friends, that is . . . It's disgusting what she does, that young girl. She has no shame! Oh, that reminds me, Mme. Ouimet. I saw your Michel the other day . . .

ROSE:

Not with that slut!

LISETTE:

I'm afraid so.

ROSE:

Not my Michel. You must be mistaken.

LISETTE:

I beg your pardon, but the Italians are my neighbours too. They were out on the front balcony.

DES-NEIGES:

It's true, Mme. Ouimet, I saw them myself. And they were necking like crazy.

ROSE:

The little bastard! As if one pig in the family wasn't enough. He's just like his old man. Can't even watch a girl on TV without getting a . . . Without getting all worked up. Goddamn sex! They never get enough. They're all the same in that family, they . . .

GABRIELLE:

Rose, you don't have to tell the whole world . . .

LISETTE:

But we're very concerned . . .

DES-NEIGES
AND MARIE-ANGE:

Yes, we are . . .

YVETTE:

To get back to my daughter's honeymoon . . .

GERMAINE: *entering*

Here I am, girls!

Greetings, "how are you's," etc.

Well, what have you all been talking about?

ROSE:

Oh, Mme. Longpré was telling us about her daughter's honeymoon.

GERMAINE:

Really! *To YVETTE*. Hello, dear . . . *To ROSE*. And what did she say?

ROSE:

Oh, they had a real nice trip. They met all these people. They were on a boat, you know, visiting some islands. The Canary Islands. They went fishing . . . My God, she says they caught fish this big. They ran into some couples they knew . . . Old friends of Claudette's. They all came back together and, oh yes, they stopped over in New York. Mme. Longpré has just been giving us all the details . . .

YVETTE:

Well . . .

ROSE:

Eh, Mme. Longpré, isn't that right?

YVETTE:

Well, as a matter of fact . . .

GERMAINE:
> Mme. Longpré, be sure to tell your daughter that I wish her all the best. We weren't invited to the wedding, you know, but we wish her well all the same.

> *There is an embarrassed silence.*

GABRIELLE:
> Hey! It's almost seven o'clock! The rosary!

GERMAINE:
> Dear God, my novena for Ste-Thérèse. I'll get Linda's radio.

> *She goes out.*

ROSE:
> What does she want with Ste-Thérèse after winning all that?

DES-NEIGES:
> Maybe she's having a rough time with her kids . . .

GABRIELLE:
> No, she would have told me . . .

GERMAINE: *from the bedroom*
> Goddamn it! Where did she put that thing?

ROSE:
> I don't know, Gaby. Our sister keeps things to herself sometimes.

GABRIELLE:
> Not with me. She tells me everything. You, you're such a blabbermouth . . .

ROSE:

What do you mean, blabbermouth? My mouth's nowhere near as big as yours!

GABRIELLE:

Come on! You can't keep a secret for five minutes.

ROSE:

Why, Gabrielle Jodoin . . . If you think . . .

LISETTE:

Wasn't it you, Mme. Ouimet, who said we didn't come here to quarrel?

ROSE:

Hey, you mind your own business. Besides, I didn't say "quarrel." I said "fight."

GERMAINE comes back in with a radio.

GERMAINE:

What's going on? I can hear you down at the other end of the hall!

GABRIELLE:

Oh, it's our sister again . . .

GERMAINE:

Settle down, eh, Rose! I don't want any fighting tonight.

ROSE:

There, you see! In our family we say "fight."

GERMAINE turns on the radio. We hear a voice saying the rosary. All the women get down on their knees. After a few "Hail Marys" a great racket is heard outside. The women scream and run to the door.

GERMAINE:

Oh my God! It's Thérèse, my husband's sister. Her mother-in-law just fell down three flights of stairs!

ROSE:

Did you hurt yourself, Mme. Dubuc?

GABRIELLE:

Rose, shut up! She must be half dead!

THERESE: *from a distance*

Are you all right, Mme. Dubuc? *A faint moan is heard.* Wait a minute. Let me get the wheelchair off you. Is that better? Now I'm gonna help you get back in your chair. Come on, Mme. Dubuc, make a little effort. Don't stay so limp! Come on, get up there!

DES-NEIGES:

Here, Mme. Dubuc. Let me give you a hand.

THERESE:

Thank you, Mlle. Verrette. You're very kind.

The other women come back into the room.

ROSE:

Germaine, shut off the radio. I'm a nervous wreck!

GERMAINE:

What about my novena?

ROSE:

How far have you gotten?

GERMAINE:

I'm only up to seven, but I promised to do nine.

ROSE:

So, pick it up tomorrow and you'll be finished on
Saturday.

GERMAINE:

It's not for nine days. It's for nine weeks.

> *THERESE DUBUC and DES-NEIGES VERRETTE ente*
> *with OLIVINE DUBUC, who is in a wheelchair.*

My God, she wasn't hurt bad, I hope?

THERESE:

No, no, she's used to it. She's always falling out of
her chair. Whew! I'm all out of breath. It's no joke,
dragging that thing up three flights of stairs. You
got something to drink, Germaine?

GERMAINE:

Gaby, give Thérèse a glass of water.

> *She approaches OLIVINE DUBUC.*

And how are you today, Mme. Dubuc?

THERESE:

Don't get too close, Germaine. She's been biting
lately.

> *In fact, OLIVINE DUBUC tries to bite*
> *GERMAINE's hand.*

GERMAINE:

My God, you're right! She's dangerous! How long
has she been doing that?

THERESE:

Would you mind turning off the radio, Germaine?
It's driving me nuts. I can't take it after what's just
happened.

GERMAINE reluctantly shuts off the radio.

GERMAINE:
> It's alright, Thérèse, I understand.

THERESE:
> Honestly, you don't know what it's like, Germaine.
> It's killing me. Imagine having your mother-in-law on
> your back all the time. It's not that I don't like her,
> the poor old thing. Don't get me wrong. She deserves
> a lot of sympathy. But her health, it's so unpredict-
> able. I've got to watch her day and night.

DES-NEIGES:
> How come she's out of the hospital?

THERESE:
> Well, you see, Mlle, Verrette, three months ago my
> husband got a raise, so welfare stopped paying for
> his mother. If she'd stay there, we would have had
> to pay all the bills ourselves.

MARIE-ANGE:
> My, my, my . . .

YVETTE:
> That's awful.

DES-NEIGES:
> Dreadful!

> *During THERESE's speech, GERMAINE opens
> the boxes and distributes the stamps and books.*

THERESE:
> What else could we do? We had to take her out.
> She's such a burden, ladies. Do you know she's
> ninety-three years old? It's like having a baby in the
> house. She's gotta be dressed, undressed, washed . . .

DES-NEIGES:
    God forbid!

YVETTE:
    You poor thing.

THERESE:
    It's no fun, believe me. Why only this morning
    I had to go shopping. I said to Paul . . . He's my
    youngest . . . "Mama's going out, so you stay here and
    take care of Granny." Can you believe it? When I
    got home, Mme. Dubuc had dumped a quart of
    molasses all over herself and was playing in it like a
    kid. Of course, Paul was nowhere to be seen. I had
    to clean the table, the floor, the wheelchair . . .

GERMAINE:
    What about Mme. Dubuc?

THERESE:
    I left her like that for the rest of the afternoon. And
    why not? If she's gonna act like a baby, I'm gonna
    treat her like one. Do you realize I have to spoon-
    feed her?

GERMAINE:
    My poor Thérèse. How I feel for you.

DES-NEIGES:
    You're too good, Thérèse.

GABRIELLE:
    Much too good. I agree.

THERESE:
    Well, that's life. We all have our crosses to bear.

MARIE-ANGE:
    If you ask me, Thérèse, you've got a heavy one!

THERESE:

Oh well, I don't complain. I just tell myself that our Lord is good and He's gonna help me get through.

LISETTE:

I can't bear it. It makes you want to weep.

THERESE:

Now, Mme. de Courval, don't get carried away.

DES-NEIGES:

Mme. Dubuc, all I can say is you're a real saint.

GERMAINE:

Well, now that you've all got stamps and booklets, I'll put a little water in some saucers and we can get started, eh? We don't want to spend the whole night yacking.

She fills a few saucers and passes them around. The women start pasting the stamps in the books. GERMAINE goes out on the balcony.

Linda! Linda! Richard, have you seen Linda? . . . The little brat! She's got a lot of nerve to sit there and drink Coke while I'm slaving away. Be an angel, will you, and tell her to come home right away? And you come see Mme. Lauzon tomorrow. She'll give you some peanuts if there's any left, okay? Go on now and tell her to come home this minute.

She comes back inside.

The little bitch. She promised to stay home.

MARIE-ANGE:

Kids are all the same.

THERESE:

You can say that again! They got no respect.

GABRIELLE:

Don't tell me about it. It's gotten so bad in our
house I can hardly stand it. You wouldn't recognize
my Raymond. He's changed something awful . . . Ever
since he started college. Walks around with his nose
in the air like he's too good for us, speaks Latin
at the dinner table, makes us listen to his crazy music
all day long. Can you imagine, classical music in the
middle of the afternoon? And if we don't feel like
watching his stupid TV concerts, the little bugger
has hysterics. If there's one thing I can't stand, it's
classical music.

ROSE:

Ah! You're not the only one.

THERESE:

I agree. It drives me crazy. Clink! Clank! Bang!
Bong!

GABRIELLE:

Of course, Raymond says we don't understand it.
As if there was anything to understand! Just because
he's learning all sorts of nonsense at college, he thinks
he can treat us like dirt. I've got half a mind to yank
him out and put him to work!

ALL THE WOMEN:

Kids are so ungrateful! Kids are so ungrateful!

GERMAINE:

Be sure to fill the books, eh, girls? Stamps on every
page.

ROSE:

Relax, Germaine, you'd think we'd never done it
before.

YVETTE:

Isn't it getting a little warm in here? Why don't we open the window?

GERMAINE:

No, no, not with the stamps. It'll make a draft.

ROSE:

Come on, Germaine, they're not birds. They won't fly away. Oh, speaking of birds, last Sunday I went to see Bernard, my oldest. Well, you've never seen anything like it. Birds all over the place. In fact, the house is one big bird cage. And it's all her doing, you know. She's nuts about birds! And she won't kill any of them. Too soft-hearted, she says. Well, fine. Maybe she's soft-hearted, but surely to God there's a limit. Listen to this, it's a scream.

Spotlight on ROSE OUIMET.

ROSE:

The woman's nuts, no kidding. I joke about it, but really, it's not funny. Anyway, last Easter, Bernard picked up this bird cage for the kids. Some guy down at the tavern needed money, so he sold it to him cheap . . . Well, the minute he got it in the house, she went bananas. Fell head over heels in love with his birds. No kidding. She took better care of them than she did her kids. Of course, in no time at all the females were laying eggs . . . And when they started to hatch, Manon, she thought they were so cute. She didn't have the heart to get rid of them. You've got to be crazy, eh? So she kept them! The whole flock! God knows how many she's got. I never tried to count 'em . . . But, believe me, every time I set foot in the place I nearly go out of my mind! But wait, you haven't heard anything yet. Everyday around two, she opens up the cage and out come her stupid birds. What happens? They fly all

31

over the house. They shit all over everything, including
us and we run around after them cleaning it all up.
Of course, when it's time to get them back in the
cage, they don't want to go. They're having too much
fun! So Manon starts screaming at the kids, "Catch
the little birdies now. Mama's too tired." And the
little monsters go charging after the birds and the
place is a bloody circus. Me, I get the hell out! I go
sit on the balcony and wait till they've all been
caught.

The women laugh.

And those kids! God, what brats! Oh, I like them
okay. They're my grandchildren. But Jesus, do they
drive me nuts. Our kids weren't like that. Say what
you like. Young people today, they don't know how
to bring up their kids!

GERMAINE:
You said it!

YVETTE:
That's for sure.

ROSE:
I mean, take the bathroom. Now we wouldn't have
let out kids play in there. Well, you should have seen
it on Sunday. The kids went in there like they were
just going about their business and in no time flat
they'd made a mess like you have never seen. Me, I
didn't say a word! Manon says I talk too much as it
is. But I could hear them alright and they were
getting on my nerves but good. You know what
they were doing? Playing with the toilet paper.
That's right. They'd unrolled it, the whole goddamn
thing. Manon just sat there yelling, "Hey, you kids,
Mama's gonna get angry." A lot of good that does.
They didn't pay any attention. They kept right on

going. I would've skinned 'em alive, the little buggers. And were they having a ball! Bruno, the youngest . . . Can you imagine calling a kid Bruno? I still can't get over it . . . Anyway, Bruno climbed into the bathtub fully dressed and all rolled up in toilet paper and turned on the water. Listen, he was laughing so hard he nearly drowned! He was making boats out of soggy paper and the water was running all over the place. A real flood! Well, I had to do something. I mean, enough is enough. So I gave them a good licking and sent them off to bed.

YVETTE:
That's exactly what they needed!

ROSE:
Their mother raised a stink, of course, but I'll be damned if I was gonna let them carry on like that. Manon, the dim-wit, she just sits there peeling potatoes and listening to the radio. Oh, she's a winner, that one! But I guess she's happy. The only thing she worries about is her birds. Poor Bernard! At times I really feel sorry for him, being married to that. He should have stayed home with me. He was a lot better off . . .

She bursts out laughing.

YVETTE:
Isn't she a riot! There's no holding her back.

GABRIELLE:
Yeah, it's always fun to go to a party with Rose.

ROSE:
When it's time to laugh, you might as well have a good one. That's what I say. Every story has a funny side, you know. Even the sad ones . . .

THERESE:

>You're lucky you can say that, Mme. Ouimet. It's
>not everyone . . .

DES-NEIGES:

>We understand, dear. It must be hard for you to
>laugh with all your troubles. You're far too good,
>Mme. Dubuc! You're always thinking of others . . .

ROSE:

>That's right, you should think of yourself sometimes.
>You never go out.

THERESE:

>I don't have time! When would you have me go out?
>I have to take care of her . . . Even if there was
>nothing else . . .

GERMAINE:

>Don't tell me there's something else, Thérèse.

THERESE:

>If you only knew! Now that my husband's making
>some money, the family thinks we're millionaires.
>Why only yesterday my sister-in-law's cousin came to
>the house with her hand out. Well, you know me.
>When she told me her story, I just felt awful. So I let
>her have some old clothes I didn't need anymore . . .
>Ah, she was so happy . . . And she was crying . . . She
>even tried to kiss my hands.

DES-NEIGES:

>I'm not surprised. You deserve it!

MARIE-ANGE:

>Mme. Dubuc, I really do admire you.

THERESE:

>Oh, don't say that . . .

DES-NEIGES:

No, no, no. It's true. You deserve it.

LISETTE:

It certainly is, Mme. Dubuc. You deserve our admiration and I assure you, I shan't forget you in my prayers.

THERESE:

Well, I always say, "If God has placed poor people on this earth, they gotta be encouraged."

GERMAINE:

When you're through filling your books there instead of piling them on the table, why don't we put them back in the box? . . . Rose, give me a hand. We'll take all the empty books out and put the full ones in . . .

ROSE:

Good idea. My God! What a lot of books! We gotta fill all them tonight?

GERMAINE:

Sure, why not? Besides, everyone's not here yet, so we . . .

DES-NEIGES:

Who else is coming, Mme. Lauzon?

GERMAINE:

Rhéauna Bibeau and Angéline Sauvé are gonna stop by after the funeral parlour. One of Mlle. Bibeau's old girlfriends has a daughter whose husband died. Baril, I think his name was . . .

YVETTE:

Not Rosaire Baril.

GERMAINE:

Yeah, I think that's it . . .

YVETTE:

But I knew him well! I used to go out with him
for Godsake. How do you like that. I'd have been
a widow today.

GABRIELLE:

Guess what, girls? I got the eight mistakes in last
Saturday's paper. It's the first time I ever got 'em
all and I've been trying for six months . . . I sent in
the answer . . .

YVETTE:

Did you win anything yet?

GABRIELLE:

Do I look like someone who's ever won anything?

THERESE:

Hey, Germaine, what are you going to do with all
these stamps?

GERMAINE:

Didn't I tell you? I'm going to re-decorate the house.
Wait a minute . . . Where did I put the catalogue? . . .
Ah, here it is. Look at that, Thérèse. I'm gonna have
all that for nothing.

THERESE:

For nothing! You mean it's not going to cost you a
cent?

GERMAINE:

Not a cent! You know, these contests are terrific.

LISETTE:

That's not what Mme. Brouillette said a while ago . . .

GERMAINE:

What do you mean?

MARIE-ANGE:

Mme. de Courval, really!

ROSE:

Well, come on, Mme, Brouillette. Don't be afraid to
say what you think. You said earlier you don't like
the contests because only one family wins.

MARIE-ANGE:

Well, it's true! All these lotteries and contests are
unfair. I'm against them.

GERMAINE:

Just because you never won anything.

MARIE-ANGE:

Maybe so, but they're still not fair.

GERMAINE:

Not fair, my eye! You're jealous, that's all You said
so yourself the minute you walked in here. Well, I
don't like jealous people, Mme Brouillette. I don't
like them one bit! In fact, if you really want to
know, I can't *stand* them.

MARIE-ANGE:

Well! If that's how you're going to be, I'm leaving.

GERMAINE:

Now, wait a minute! I'm sorry . . . I'm all nerves
tonight. I don't know what I'm saying. Let's just
forget it, okay? You have every right to your
opinions. Every right. Just sit back down and
keep pasting, okay?

ROSE:

Our sister here's afraid of losing one of her workers.

GABRIELLE:

> Shut up, Rose! You're always sticking your nose where it don't belong.

ROSE:

> What's eating you, for Chrissake? Can't I even open my mouth?

MARIE-ANGE:

> Alright, I'll stay. But I still don't like them.

> > *From this point on, MARIE-ANGE BROUIL-LETTE will steal all the books she fills. The others will see what she's doing right from the start, except for GERMAINE, obviously, and will decide to follow suit.*

LISETTE:

> Well, I figured out the mystery charade in last month's Châtelaine. It was very easy . . . My first syllable is a Persian king . . .

ROSE:

> Onassis?

LISETTE:

> No, a *Persian* king . . . It's a "shah" . . .

ROSE:

> That's a Persian?

LISETTE:

> Why, of course . . .

ROSE: *laughing*
> That's his tough luck!

LISETTE:

> My second is for killing bugs . . . No one? . . . Oh well, "Raid" . . .

ROSE:

My husband's a worm. Do you think it would work on him? . . . She's really nuts with all this stuff, eh?

LISETTE:

And the whole thing is a social game . . .

ROSE:

The bottle!

GABRIELLE:

Rose, will you shut up for Godsake!   *to LISETTE*
Scrabble?

LISETTE:

Oh, come now, it's simple . . . Shah-raid . . .
Charade!

YVETTE:

Ah . . . What's a charade?

LISETTE:

Of course, I figured it out in no time . . . It was so easy . . .

YVETTE:

So, did you win anything?

LISETTE:

Oh, I didn't bother to send it in. I just did it for the challenge . . . Besides, do I look like I need such things?

ROSE:

Well, I like mystery words, hidden words, crosswords, turned-around words, bilingual words. You know. All that stuff with words. It's my specialty. I'm a real champ, you know. I've broken all the records!
Never miss a contest . . . Costs me two bucks a week just for stamps!

YVETTE:
So, did you win yet?

ROSE: *looking at GERMAINE*
Do I look like somebody who's ever won anything?

THERESE:
Mme. Dubuc, will you kindly let go of my saucer? . . .
There! Now you've done it. You've spilled it! That's
the last straw!

> *She socks her mother-in-law on the head and the
> latter settles down a little.*

GABRIELLE:
You don't fool around, do you? Aren't you afraid
you'll hurt her?

THERESE:
No, no. She's used to it. It's the only way to shut her
up. My husband figured it out. If you give her a
good bash on the head, it seems to knock her out
a while. That way she stays in her corner and we get
some peace.

> *Blackout.*

> *Spotlight on YVETTE LONGPRE.*

YVETTE:
When my daughter Claudette got back from her
honeymoon, she gave me the top part of her wedding
cake. I was so proud! It's such a lovely piece. A
miniature sanctuary all made of icing. It's got a red
velvet stairway leading up to a platform and on top
of that platform stand the bride and groom. Two
little dolls all dressed up like newly weds. There's
even a priest to bless them and behind him there's an
altar. It's *all* icing. I've never seen anything quite so
beautiful. Of course, we paid a lot for the cake.

After all, six levels! It wasn't *all* cake though. That would have cost a fortune. Just the first two levels were cake. The rest was wood. But it's amazing, eh? You'd never have guessed. Anyway, when my daughter gave me the top part, she had it put under this glass bell. It looked so pretty, but I was afraid it would spoil . . . You know, without air. So I took my husband's glass knife . . . He's got a special knife for cutting glass . . . And I cut a hole in the top of the bell. Now the air will stay fresh and the cake won't go bad.

DES-NEIGES:

Me too. I took a stab at a contest a few weeks ago. You had to find a slogan for some bookstore . . . Hachette Bookstore or something . . . Anyway, I gave it a try . . . I came up with "Hachette will help you chop the cost of your books." Not bad, eh?

YVETTE:

Yeah, but did you win anything?

DES-NEIGES:

Do I look like somebody who's ever won anything?

GERMAINE:

By the way, Rose, I saw you cutting your grass this morning. You should get yourself a lawn-mower.

ROSE:

What for? I get along fine with scissors. Besides, it keeps me in shape.

GERMAINE:

Come on! You were puffing away like a steam engine.

ROSE:

I'm telling you, it's good for me. Anyway, I can't afford a lawn-mower. Even if I could, that's the last thing I'd buy.

GERMAINE:
>   I'll be getting a lawn-mower with my stamps . . .

DES-NEIGES:
>   She and her stamps are beginning to get on my nerves!

>   *She hides a booklet in her purse.*

ROSE:
>   Now what are you gonna do with a lawn-mower on the
>   the third floor?

GERMAINE:
>   You never know, it might come in handy. And who
>   knows. We might move someday.

DES-NEIGES:
>   I suppose she's going to tell us she needs a new house
>   to put all her new stuff in.

GERMAINE:
>   You must admit, we'll probably need a bigger place . . .

>   *DES-NEIGES VERRETTE, MARIE-ANGE*
>   *BROUILLETTE and THERESE DUBUC all*
>   *hide two or three books each.*

>   Rose, if you want, you can borrow my lawn-mower.

ROSE:
>   Hell, no! I might bust it. I'd be collecting stamps for
>   the next two years just to pay you back.

>   *The women laugh.*

GERMAINE:
>   Don't be smart!

MARIE-ANGE:

Isn't she something! Can you beat that!

THERESE:

Hey, I forgot to tell you. I guessed the mystery voice on the radio . . . It was Duplessis . . . My husband figured it out 'cause it was an old voice. I sent twenty-five letters just to be sure they get it. And for extra luck, I signed my youngest boy's name, Paul Dubuc . . .

YVETTE:

Did you win anything yet?

THERESE: *looking at GERMAINE*

Do I look like someone who's ever won anything?

GABRIELLE:

Say, do you know what my husband's gonna get me for my birthday?

ROSE:

Same as last year. Two pairs of nylons.

GABRIELLE:

No sir-ee! A fur coat. Of course, it's not real fur, but who cares? I don't think real fur's worth buying anymore. The synthetics they make nowadays are just as nice. In fact, sometimes nicer.

LISETTE:

Oh, I disagree . . .

ROSE:

Sure, we all know who's got a fat mink stole!

LISETTE:

Well, if you ask me, there's no substitute for authentic, genuine fur. Incidentally, I'll be getting a new stole in the autumn. The one I have now is three

years old and it's starting to look . . . Well, a bit tatty.
Mind you, it's still mink, but . . .

ROSE:

Shut your mouth, you bloody liar! We know goddamn well your husband's up to his ass in debt
because of your mink stoles and your trips to Europe!
You're not fooling us with that shit about being rich.
You've got no more money than the rest of us!

LISETTE:

Mme. Jodoin, if your husband wants to buy my stole,
he can have it for a good price. Then you'll have real
mink. After all, between friends . . .

YVETTE:

You know the inflated objects game in the paper, the
one where you're supposed to guess what the objects
are? Well, I guessed them. There was a screw, a
screw-driver and some kind of bent up hook.

THE OTHERS:

So . . .

YVETTE sits down.

GERMAINE:

You know Daniel, Mme. Robitaille's little boy? He
fell off the second floor balcony the other day. Not
even a scratch! How do you like that, eh?

MARIE-ANGE:

Yes, and he landed on Mme. Turgeon's hammock.
And Monsieur Turgeon was in it at the time . . .

GERMAINE:

That's right. He's in hospital for three months.

DES-NEIGES:

Speaking of accidents reminds me, I heard a joke the
other day . . .

ROSE:

Well, aren't you gonna tell us?

DES-NEIGES:

Oh, I couldn't. It's too racy . . .

ROSE:

Come on, Mlle. Verrette! It won't be the first.

DES-NEIGES:

No. I'm too embarrassed. I don't know why, but I am . . .

GABRIELLE:

Don't be such a tease, Mlle. Verrette. You know darn well you're gonna tell us anyway . . .

DES-NEIGES:

Well . . . Alright . . . There was this nun who got raped in an alley . . .

ROSE:

Sounds good!

DES-NEIGES:

And the next morning they found her lying in the yard, a terrible mess, her habit pulled over her head, moaning away . . . So this reporter comes running over and he says to her, "Excuse me, Sister, but could you tell us something about this terrible thing that's happened to you?" Well, she opens her eyes, looks up at him and in a very small voice she says, "Again, please."

> *All the women burst out laughing except for LISETTE DE COURVAL who appears scandalized.*

ROSE:

I'll be dammed. She's fantastic! I haven't heard such a good one for ages. I'm gonna wet my pants, for Chrissake. Mlle. Verrette, where in the world do you get them?

GABRIELLE:

Oh, you know. From her travelling salesman . . .

DES-NEIGES:

Mme. Jodoin, please!

ROSE:

That's right too. Her travelling salesman . . .

LISETTE:

I don't understand.

GABRIELLE:

Mlle. Verrette has a travelling salesman who comes to sell her brushes every month. I think she likes him more than his brushes.

DES-NEIGES:

Mme. Jodoin!

ROSE:

Well, I know one thing. Mlle, Verrette has more brushes than anyone in the neighbourhood. Hey, I saw your boyfriend the other day . . . He was sitting in the restaurant . . . He must have been to see you, eh?

DES-NEIGES:

I assure you, there's nothing between us. If that's what you're thinking . . .

ROSE:

That's what they all say.

DES-NEIGES:

Honestly, Mme. Ouimet, you go too far! Monsieur Simard is a very nice man.

ROSE:

Yeah, but who's to say you're a nice lady? Now, now, Mlle. Verrette, don't get angry. I'm only pulling your leg.

DES-NEIGES:

Then don't say things like that. Of course, I'm a nice lady and a thoroughly respectable one! By the way, the last time he was over, Henri . . . Er . . . Monsieur Simard was telling me about a project he has in mind . . . And he asked me to extend you all an invitation. He wants me to organize a demonstration next week . . . At my house. He chose me because he knows my house . . . It'd be for a week Sunday, right after the rosary. I need at least ten people if I'm gonna get my present . . . You know, they give away those fancy cups to the one who holds the demonstration . . . You should see them, they're gorgeous. They're souvenirs he brought back from Niagara Falls . . . They probably cost a fortune.

ROSE:

Sure, we'll go to that, eh, girls? I've always been crazy about demonstrations. Any door prizes?

DES-NEIGES:

I don't know. I suppose there might be. Anyway, I'll be giving a lunch . . .

ROSE:

That's more than you get around here. We'll be lucky to see a glass of water!

OLIVINE DUBUC tries to bite her daughter-in-law.

47

THERESE:

> Mme. Dubuc, if you don't stop that I'm gonna lock
> you in the bathroom and you can stay there for the
> rest of the evening.

> *Blackout.*

> *Spotlight on DES-NEIGES VERRETTE.*

DES-NEIGES:

> The first time I saw him I thought he was ugly . . .
> It's true. He's not that good-looking. When I opened
> the door, he took off his hat and said, "Would you
> be interested in buying some brushes, Madame?" I
> slammed the door in his face. I never let a man in the
> house! Who knows what might happen . . . The only
> one who gets in is the paper boy. He's still too young
> to get any wrong ideas. Well, a month later my
> friend with the brushes came back. There was a
> terrible snowstorm outside, so I let him stand in the
> hall. Once he was in the house, I began to get very
> frightened, but I told myself he didn't look too
> dangerous even if he wasn't very handsome . . . He
> always looks so smart . . . Not a hair out of place . . .
> He's a real gentlemen . . . And so polite! Well, he sold
> me a couple of brushes and then he showed me his
> catalogue. There was one that I wanted, but he didn't
> have it with him, so he said I could place an order.
> Ever since then, he's come back once a month.
> Sometimes I don't buy a thing. He just comes in and
> we chat for a while. He's such a nice man. When he
> speaks, you forget that he's plain. And he knows so
> many interesting things! The man must travel all
> over the province! I think . . . I think I'm in love
> with him . . . I know it's silly. I only see him once a
> month, but it's so nice when we're together. I'm
> so happy when he comes. I've never felt this
> way before. Never. Men never paid much attention
> to me. I've always been . . . Unattached. But he tells me

48

about his trips, and all kinds of stories . . . Sometimes
they're a bit risqué, but honestly, they're so funny!
I must admit, I've always liked stories that are a bit
off-colour . . . And it's good for you to tell them
sometimes. Not all his jokes are dirty, mind you. Lots
of them are clean. And it's only lately that he's been
telling me the spicey ones. Sometimes I blush, they're
so dirty. The last time he came he took my hand
when I blushed. I nearly went out of my mind. My
insides went all funny when he put his big hand on
mine. I need him so badly! I don't want him to go
away! Sometimes, just sometimes, I dream about
him. I dream . . . That we're married. I need him to
come and see me. He's the first man that ever cared
about me. I don't want to lose him! I don't want
to! If he goes away, I'll be all alone again and I need
. . . To love someone . . .

> *She lowers her eyes and murmurs.*

I need a man.

> *The lights come on again. LINDA LAUZON,*
> *GINETTE MENARD and LISE PAQUETTE enter.*

GERMAINE:
Well, look who's here. It's about time!

LINDA:
I was at the restaurant.

GERMAINE:
I know you were at the restaurant. You keep hang-
ing around there, you're gonna end up like your
Aunt Pierrette . . . in a whore house.

LINDA:
Lay off, Ma! You're making a stink over nothing.

GERMAINE:

I asked you to stay home . . .

LINDA:

Look, I went to get cigarettes and I ran into Lise
and Ginette . . .

GERMAINE:

That's no excuse. You knew I was having company.
You should have come home right away. You do it
on purpose, Linda. You do it just to make me angry.
You want me to lose my temper in front of all my
friends? Is that it? You want me to swear in public?
Well, Christ Almighty, you've succeeded! But don't
think you're off the hook yet, Linda Lauzon. I'll
take care of you later.

ROSE:

This is no time to bawl her out, Germaine!

GABRIELLE:

Rose, you mind your own business.

LINDA:

My God! I'm only a few minutes late. It's not the
end of the world!

LISE:

It's our fault, Mme. Lauzon.

GINETTE:

Yeah, it's our fault.

GERMAINE:

I know it's your fault. And I've told Linda a hundred
times not to run around with tramps. But you think
she gives a damn? Sometimes I'd like to strangle her!

ROSE:

>Now, Germaine . . .

GABRIELLE:

>Rose, I told you to stay out of this! Do you hear?
>It's their business. It's got nothing to do with you.

ROSE:

>Will you get off my back? What's with you anyway?
>Linda's getting bawled out and she hasn't done a
>goddamn thing!

GABRIELLE:

>It's none of our business!

LINDA:

>Leave her alone, Aunt Gaby. She's only trying to
>defend me.

GABRIELLE:

>Don't you tell *me* what to do! I'm your Godmother!

GERMAINE:

>You see what she's like! Day in and day out! I never
>brought her up to act this way.

ROSE:

>Now that you mention it, how *do* you raise your
>kids?

GERMAINE:

>Hah! You should talk! . . . Your kids . . .

LINDA:

>Go on, Aunt Rose. Give it to her good. Really tell
>her! You're the only one who can.

GERMAINE:

>What's come over you that you side with Aunt Rose all of a sudden? Have you forgotten what you said when she phoned a while ago, eh? Come on, Linda, tell Aunt Rose what you said about her.

LINDA:

>That was different . . .

ROSE:

>Why, what did she say?

GERMAINE:

>Well, she answered the phone when you called, right? And she was too rude to say, "One moment, please," so I told her to be more polite with you . . .

LINDA:

>Will you shut up, Ma! That has nothing to do with it.

ROSE:

>I want to know what you said, Linda.

LINDA:

>It's not important. I was mad at her.

GERMAINE:

>She said, "It's only Aunt Rose. Why should I be polite to her?"

ROSE:

>Well, of all the nerve! You said that?

LINDA:

>I told you. I was mad at her!

ROSE:

>I'd never have thought that of you, Linda. There, you've let me down. You've really let me down.

GABRIELLE:

Let them fight it out themselves, Rose.

ROSE:

You bet I'll let 'em fight. Go on, Germaine. Give it
to her good, the little brat! You wanna know something, Linda? Your mother's right. If you're not
careful, you'll end up like your Aunt Pierrette. I've
got a good mind to slap you right in the face!

GERMAINE:

Just you try it! No one lays a hand on my kids, you
hear? If they need a beating, I'll give it to them.
Nobody else!

THERESE:

For Godsake, stop the bickering. I'm too tired!

DES-NEIGES:

Lord, yes, you're wearing us out.

THERESE:

You want to wake up my mother-in-law and get her
going again?

GERMAINE:

Look, she's your problem, not mine! Why didn't
you leave her at home?

THERESE:

Germaine Lauzon!

GABRIELLE:

Well, she's right. You don't go out to parties with a
ninety-three year old cripple.

LISETTE:

Mme. Jodoin, didn't I just hear you tell your sister to
mind her own business?

GABRIELLE:

>Keep your big nose out of this, you stuck up bitch!
>Shut your yap and keep pasting or I'll shut it for you.

>*LISETTE DE COURVAL gets up.*

LISETTE:

>Gabrielle Jodoin!

>*OLIVINE DUBUC spills the saucer she has been
>playing with.*

THERESE:

>Mme. Dubuc, for Godsake!

GERMAINE:

>Goddamn it, my tablecloth!

ROSE:

>She's soaked me, the old bag!

THERESE:

>That's not true! You weren't even close!

ROSE:

>Sure, call me a liar right to my face!

THERESE:

>You're a liar!

GERMAINE:

>Look out, she's falling out of her chair!

DES-NEIGES:

>Good Lord, she's on the floor again!

THERESE:

>Somebody give me a hand.

ROSE:
>   Not me, that's for sure!

GABRIELLE:
>   Pick her up yourself.

DES-NEIGES:
>   Here, I'll help you, Mme. Dubuc.

THERESE:
>   Thanks, Mlle. Verrette.

GERMAINE:
>   Listen, Linda, you better stay out of my way for
>   the rest of the evening.

LINDA:
>   Fine. We'll go back to the restaurant.

GERMAINE:
>   You leave now and you won't set foot in this house
>   again, you hear?

LINDA:
>   Sure, I've heard it a thousand times.

LISE:
>   Cut it out, Linda . . .

THERESE:
>   For Godsake, Mme. Dubuc, don't stay so limp. You
>   do it on purpose.

MARIE-ANGE:
>   I'll hold the chair.

THERESE:
>   Thank you . . .

ROSE:
> If it was me, I'd take that lousy chair and . . .

GABRIELLE:
> Stop it, Rose!

THERESE:
> Whew! What I go through . . .

GABRIELLE:
> Hey, will you get a load of de Courval, still pasting
> her stamps . . . The bloody snob. As if nothing had
> happened! I guess we're not good enough for her.

> *Blackout.*

> *Spotlight on LISETTE DE COURVAL.*

LISETTE:
> It's like living in a barnyard. Léopold told me not to
> come and he was right. I should have stayed at home.
> We don't belong with these people. Once you've
> tasted life on an ocean liner and you have to come
> back to this, well . . . It's enough to make you weep
> . . . I can still see myself, stretched out on the deck
> chair, a Book of the Month in my lap . . . And that
> lieutenant who was giving me the eye . . . My
> husband says he wasn't, but he didn't see what *I* saw
> . . . Mmmm . . . That was some man. Maybe I should
> have encouraged him a little more . . . *She sighs.*
> . . . And Europe! Everyone there is so refined! So
> much more polite than here. You'd never meet a
> Germaine Lauzon in Europe. Never. Only people of
> substance. In Paris, you know, everyone speaks so
> beautifully and there they talk *real* French . . . Not
> like here . . . I despise everyone of them. I'll never
> set foot in this place again! Léopold was right about
> these people. These people are *cheap*. We shouldn't

be with them. We shouldn't talk about them . . . They should be hidden away somewhere. They don't know how to live! We broke away from this and we must never go back. Dear God, they make me so ashamed!

The lights come back up.

LINDA:

I've had it. I'm leaving . . .

GERMAINE:

Like hell you are! I'm warning you, Linda . . .

LINDA:

"I'm warning you, Linda!" Is that all you know how to say?

LISE:

Linda, don't be stupid.

GINETTE:

Come on, let's stay.

LINDA:

No, I'm leaving. I've listened to enough crap for one night.

GERMAINE:

Linda, I forbid you to leave!

VOICE OF A
NEIGHBOUR:

Will you stop screaming up there. We can't hear ourselves think!

ROSE goes out on the balcony.

ROSE:

Hey, you! Get back in your house.

NEIGHBOUR:
>I wasn't talking to you!

ROSE:
>Oh yes, you were. I'm just as loud as the rest of them!

GABRIELLE:
>Rose, get in here!

DES-NEIGES: *referring to the neighbour*
>Don't pay any attention to her.

NEIGHBOUR:
>You want me to call the cops?

ROSE:
>Go ahead and call 'em. We need a few men up here.

GERMAINE:
>Rose Ouimet, get back in this house! And you, Linda . . .

LINDA:
>I'm leaving. See ya!

>*She goes out with GINETTE and LISE.*

GERMAINE:
>She's gone! Walked right out! I can't believe it! She wants to kill me, that kid. I'm gonna smash something. I'm gonna smash something!

ROSE:
>Germaine, control yourself.

GERMAINE:
>Making a fool of me in front of everyone!

She starts sobbing.

My own daughter . . . I'm so ashamed!

GABRIELLE:
Come on, Germaine. It's not that bad . . .

LINDA'S VOICE:
Hey, if it isn't Mlle. Sauvé. How are you doing?

ANGELINE'S VOICE:
Hello, sweetheart, how are you?

ROSE:
Germaine, they're here. Blow your nose and stop crying.

LINDA'S VOICE:
Not bad, thanks.

RHEAUNA'S VOICE:
Where are you off to?

LINDA'S VOICE:
I was gonna go to the restaurant, but now that you're here, I think I'll stay.

LINDA, GINETTE and LISE enter with ANGELINE and RHEAUNA.

ANGELINE:
Hello, everybody.

RHEAUNA:
Hello.

THE OTHERS:
Hello, hello. Come on in, how have you been . . . *etc.*

RHEAUNA:

>That's quite a climb, Mme. Lauzon. I'm all out of breath.

GERMAINE:

>Well, have a seat . . .

ROSE:

>You're out of breath? Don't worry, my sister will take care of that. She's getting an elevator with her stamps.

>>*They all laugh except RHEAUNA and ANGELINE who don't understand.*

GERMAINE:

>Very funny, Rose! Linda, go get some more chairs . . .

LINDA:

>Where? There aren't anymore.

GERMAINE:

>Go ask Mme. Bergeron if she'll lend us a few . . .

LINDA: *to the girls*

>Come on . . .

GERMAINE: *low, to LINDA*

>Okay, it's peace for now, but you wait till the others have gone . . .

LINDA:

>Look, if I came back it's because Mlle. Sauvé and Mlle. Bibeau arrived, not because of you.

>>*LINDA goes out with her friends.*

DES-NEIGES:

>Here, take my seat, Mlle. Bibeau . . .

THERESE:

    Yes, come and sit next to me . . .

MARIE-ANGE:

    Sit down here, Mlle. Bibeau . . .

ANGELINE
AND RHEAUNA:

    Thank you. Thanks very much.

RHEAUNA:

    I see you're pasting stamps.

GERMAINE:

    We sure are. A million of 'em!

RHEAUNA:

    Dear God, a million! How are you getting on?

ROSE:

    We're doing okay . . . But my tongue's paralyzed . . .

RHEAUNA:

    You've been doing it with your tongue?

GABRIELLE:

    Of course not, she's just being smart.

ROSE:

    Good old Bibeau. Right on the ball as usual!

ANGELINE:

    Why don't we give you a hand?

ROSE:

    Sure. But wouldn't you like to do it with your
    tongue?

She bursts out laughing.

GABRIELLE:
>Rose, don't be vulgar!

GERMAINE:
>So, how was the funeral parlour?

>*Blackout.*

>*Spotlight on ANGELINE and RHEAUNA.*

RHEAUNA:
>I'm telling you, it came as a shock.

ANGELINE:
>You hardly knew him though.

RHEAUNA:
>I knew his mother. So did you. Remember, we went to school together. I watched that man grow up . . .

ANGELINE:
>Such a shame. Gone just like that. And us, we're still here.

RHEAUNA:
>Ah, but not for long . . .

ANGELINE:
>Rhéauna, please . . .

RHEAUNA:
>I know what I'm talking about. You can feel it when the end is near. I've suffered. I know.

ANGELINE:

>Ah, when it comes to that, we've both had our share. I've suffered too.

RHEAUNA:

>Not like me, Angéline. Seventeen operations! A lung, a kidney, one of my breasts . . . Gone! I'm telling you, there's not much left.

ANGELINE:

>And me with my arthritis that won't let up. But Mme. . . . What's her name . . . You know, the wife of the deceased . . . She gave me a recipe . . . She says it works wonders.

RHEAUNA:

>But you've tried everything. The doctors have all told you, there's nothing you can do. There's no cure for arthritis.

ANGELINE:

>Doctors, doctors! . . . I've had enough of doctors. All they think about is money. They bleed you to death and go to California for the winter. You know, Rhéauna, the doctor said he'd get well, Monsieur . . . What was his name again? The one who died?

RHEAUNA:

>Monsieur Baril . . .

ANGELINE:

>That's it. I can never remember it. It's easy enough too. Anyhow, the doctor told Monsieur Baril that he had nothing to worry about . . . And look what happened . . . Only forty years old . . .

RHEAUNA:

>Forty years old! That's young to die.

ANGELINE:

    He sure went fast . . .

RHEAUNA:

    She told me how it happened. It's so sad . . .

ANGELINE:

    Really? I wasn't there. How did it happen?

RHEAUNA:

    When he got home from work on Monday night, she
    thought he was looking a bit strange. He was white
    as a sheet, so she asked him how he felt. He said he
    felt okay and they started supper . . . Well now, the
    kids were making a fuss at the table and Monsieur
    Baril got mad and had to punish Rolande. That's his
    daughter . . . Of course, after that, he looked like he
    was ready to drop . . . She didn't take her eyes off
    him for a second . . . But she was telling me later
    that it happened so fast she didn't have time to do a
    thing. All of a sudden he said he felt funny and over
    he went . . . His face right in the soup. That was it!

ANGELINE:

    Lord, have mercy. So sudden! I tell you, Rhéauna,
    it's frightening. It gives me the shivers.

RHEAUNA:

    Isn't it the truth? We never know when God's going
    to come for us. He said it Himself, "I'll come like a
    thief."

ANGELINE:

    Don't talk like that. It scares me. I don't want to die
    that way. I want to die in my bed . . . Have time to
    make my confession . . .

RHEAUNA:

    Oh, God forbid that I should die before confessing!
    Angéline, promise me you'll call the priest the minute
    I'm feeling weak. Promise me that.

ANGELINE:

> You know I will. You've asked me a hundred times.
> Didn't I get him there for your last attack? You had
> communion and everything.

RHEAUNA:

> I'm so afraid to die without the last rites.

ANGELINE:

> But what do you have to confess, Rhéauna?

RHEAUNA:

> Don't say that, Angéline. Don't ever say that! We're
> never too old to sin.

ANGELINE:

> If you ask me, Rhéauna, you'll go straight to heaven.
> You've got nothing to worry about. Hey! Did you
> notice Baril's daughter? The way she's changed!
> She looks like a corpse.

RHEAUNA:

> I know. Poor Rolande. She's telling everyone she
> killed her father. It was because of her that he got
> mad, you see, at supper . . . Oh, I feel so sorry for her
> . . . And her mother. What a tragedy! Such a loss
> for everyone. They'll miss him so . . .

ANGELINE:

> You're telling me . . . The father. Mind you, it's not
> as bad as the mother, but still . . .

RHEAUNA:

> True. Losing the mother is worse. You can't replace
> a mother.

ANGELINE:

> Did you see how nice he looked? . . . Like a young
> man. He was even smiling . . . I could have sworn
> he was asleep. But I still think he's better off where

he is . . . You know what they say. It's the ones who
stay behind who most deserve the pity. Him, he's
alright now . . . Ah, I still can't get over how good he
looked. Almost like he was breathing.

RHEAUNA:
Yeah! But he wasn't.

ANGELINE:
But I can't imagine why they put him in that suit . . .

RHEAUNA:
What do you mean?

ANGELINE:
Didn't you notice? He was wearing a blue suit. Now
that's not done. Not when you're dead! A blue suit
is much too light. Now, navy-blue would be fine, but
powder blue . . . Never! When you're dead, you
should be wearing a black suit.

RHEAUNA:
Maybe he didn't have one. They're not that well
off, you know.

ANGELINE:
But dear God, you can rent a black suit! And look
at Mme. Baril's sister! In green! In a funeral parlour!
And did you notice how much she's aged? She
looks years older than her sister . . .

RHEAUNA:
She is older.

ANGELINE:
Don't be silly, Rhéauna, she's younger.

RHEAUNA:
No, she isn't.

ANGELINE:

>Why sure, Rhéauna, listen! Mme. Baril is at least thirty-seven, but her sister . . .

RHEAUNA:

>Is well over forty!

ANGELINE:

>Rhéauna, she isn't!

RHEAUNA:

>She's at least forty-five . . .

ANGELINE:

>That's what I'm telling you. She's aged so much, she looks a lot older than she is . . . Listen, my sister-in-law, Rose-Aimée, is thirty-six and the two of them went to school together . . .

RHEAUNA:

>Well, anyway, it doesn't surprise me that she's aged so fast . . . What with the life she leads . . .

ANGELINE:

>You think they're true, all those stories?

RHEAUNA:

>They must be! Mme. Baril tries to hide it 'cause it's her sister . . . But the truth always comes out. It's like Mme. Lauzon and her sister, Pierrette. Now if there's one person I can't stand, it's Pierrette Guérin. A real profligate! Nothing but shame to her whole family. I tell you, Angéline, I wouldn't want to see her soul. It must be black as night.

ANGELINE:

>Now, Rhéauna, deep down inside Pierrette isn't all bad.

GERMAINE:

My sister, Pierrette, I've had nothing to do with her
for a long time now. Not after what she did. She
was so good when she was young and so pretty.
And now, she's nothing but a whore. My sisters and
I adored her. We spoiled her rotten . . . I don't
understand. I just don't understand. Papa used to
call her his little pepper pot. He was so crazy about
her, his Pierrette. When he'd take her on his knee,
you could feel how happy he was. And the rest of
us weren't even jealous . . .

ROSE:

We'd say, "She's the youngest. It's always that way.
It's the youngest who gets the attention." When she
started school, we dressed her like a princess. I was
already married, but I remember as if it were yester-
day. Oh, she was so pretty! A real Shirley Temple!
And such a good student. A lot better than me,
that's for sure. I never did a thing in school . . . Oh,
I was the class clown, eh, that's all I've ever been
good for . . . But her, the little bugger, she was
always coming home with prizes. First in French,
first in Arithmetic, first in Religion . . . Yeah, Religion!
She was pious as a nun, that kid. I tell you, the
Sisters were nuts about her! But to see her today . . .
Dear God, I almost feel sorry for her. She must need
help sometimes . . . And she must get so lonely . . .

GABRIELLE:

When she finished school, we asked her what she
wanted to do. She said she wanted to be a teacher.
She was all set to begin her training . . . And then
she met that Johnny.

**THE THREE
SISTERS:**

Goddamn Johnny! He's a devil out of hell! If she turned out the way she did, he's the one to blame. Goddamn Johnny! Goddamn Johnny!

RHEAUNA:

What do you mean, not all bad! You've got to be pretty low to do what she did. Do you know what Mme. Longpré told me about her?

ANGELINE:

No, what?

THERESE:

Ow!!!

*The lights come back up. THERESE DUBUC
gives her mother-in-law a sock on the head.*

GERMAINE:

Thérèse, knock her senseless if you have to, but do something!

THERESE:

Sure, beat her brains out! Look, I'm doing all I can to keep her quiet. I'm not about to kill her just to make you happy.

ROSE:

If it was up to me, I'd pitch her over the balcony . . .

THERESE:

What? Say that again, Rose. I didn't understand!

ROSE:

I was talking to myself.

THERESE:
>   You're scared, eh?

ROSE:
>   Me, scared?

THERESE:
>   Yes, Rose. Scared!

MARIE-ANGE:
>   Don't tell me there's gonna be another fight.

ANGELINE:
>   There's been a fight?

THERESE:
>   I'm not gonna stand for that. She insulted my
>   mother-in-law! My husband's mother!

LISETTE:
>   There they go again!

ROSE:
>   She's too old! She isn't worth bugger all!

GERMAINE:
>   Rose!

GABRIELLE:
>   Rose, that's cruel! You should be ashamed of your-
>   self!

THERESE:
>   Rose Ouimet, I'll never forgive you for what you
>   just said! Never!

ROSE:
>   Alright! Get off my back!

ANGELINE:

>Who had a fight?

ROSE:

>You've gotta know everything, don't you, Mademoiselle Sauvé? You want us to give you all the gory details.

ANGELINE:

>Mme. Ouimet! Really!

ROSE:

>Then you can go blab it all over town, eh? Isn't that it?

RHEAUNA:

>Mme. Ouimet, I don't lose my temper often, but I will not allow you to insult my friend.

MARIE-ANGE: *apart*

>I'll just grab a few while no one's looking.

GABRIELLE: *who has seen her*

>What are you doing there, Mme. Brouillette?

ROSE:

>Okay, I've said enough. I'll shut up.

MARIE-ANGE:

>Shhhh! Take these and keep quiet!

>>*LINDA, GINETTE and LISE arrive with the chairs. There is a great hullabalou. All the women change places, taking advantage of the occasion to steal more stamps.*

>Don't be silly, take them!

DES-NEIGES:

>Aren't you overdoing it?

THERESE:
>   Mme. Dubuc, hide these in your pocket . . . No!
>   Hide them, damn it!

GERMAINE:
>   You know that guy who runs the meat shop, he's a
>   real thief! . . .

>   *The door opens suddenly and PIERRETTE*
>   *GUERIN comes in.*

PIERRETTE:
>   Hi, everybody!

THE OTHERS:
>   Pierrette!

LINDA:
>   Great! It's Aunt Pierrette!

ANGELINE:
>   Oh my God, Pierrette!

GERMAINE:
>   What are you doing here? I told you I never wanted
>   to see you again.

PIERRETTE:
>   I heard that my big sister, Germaine, had won a
>   million stamps, so I decided to come over and have
>   a look. *She sees ANGELINE.* Well, I'll be goddamned!
>   Angéline! What are you doing here?

>   *Everyone looks at ANGELINE.*

>   *Blackout.*

ACT TWO

The second act begins with PIERRETTE's entrance. Hence, the last six lines of Act One are repeated now.

The door opens suddenly and PIERRETTE GUERIN comes in.

PIERRETTE:
> Hi, everybody!

THE OTHERS:
> Pierrette!

LINDA:
> Great! It's Aunt Pierrette!

ANGELINE:
> Oh my God, Pierrette!

GERMAINE:
> What are you doing here? I told you I never wanted to see you again.

PIERRETTE:
>I heard that my big sister, Germaine, had won a million stamps, so I decided to come over and have a look. *She sees ANGELINE.* Well, I'll be goddamned! Angéline! What are you doing here?

>*Everyone looks at ANGELINE.*

ANGELINE:
>My God! I'm caught.

GERMAINE:
>What do you mean, Angéline?.

GABRIELLE:
>How come you're talking to Mlle. Sauvé like that?

ROSE:
>You oughtta be ashamed!

PIERRETTE:
>Why? We're real good friends, aren't we, Géline?

ANGELINE:
>Oh! I think I'm going to faint!

>*ANGELINE pretends to faint.*

RHEAUNA:
>Good heavens, Angéline!

ROSE:
>She's dead!

RHEAUNA:
>What?

GABRIELLE:
>Don't be ridiculous! Rose, you're getting carried away again.

PIERRETTE:

> She hasn't even fainted. She's only pretending.

> *PIERRETTE approaches ANGELINE.*

GERMAINE:

> Don't you touch her!

PIERRETTE:

> Mind your own business! She's my friend.

RHEAUNA:

> What do you mean, your friend?

GERMAINE:

> Are you trying to tell us that Mlle. Sauvé is a
> friend of yours!

PIERRETTE:

> Of course she is! She comes to see me at the club
> almost every Friday night.

ALL THE
WOMEN:

> What!

RHEAUNA:

> That's impossible.

PIERRETTE:

> Ask her! Hey, Géline, isn't it true what I'm saying?
> Come on, stop playing dead and answer me.
> Angéline, we all know you're faking! Tell them.
> Isn't it true you come to the club?

ANGELINE: *after a silence*

> Yes, it's true.

RHEAUNA:

>Oh, Angéline! Angéline!

SOME OF
THE WOMEN:

>Dear God, this is dreadful!

SOME OTHER
WOMEN:

>Dear God, this is horrible!

LINDA,
GINETTE AND LISE:

>Holy shit, that's great!

>*The lights go out.*

RHEAUNA:

>Angéline! Angéline!

>*Spotlight on ANGELINE and RHEAUNA.*

ANGELINE:

>Rhéauna, you must understand . . .

RHEAUNA:

>Don't you touch me! Get away!

THE WOMEN:

>Who would have thought . . . Such a horrible thing!

RHEAUNA:

>I'd never have thought this of you. You, in a club.
>And every Friday night! It can't be true.

ANGELINE:

>I don't do anything wrong, Rhéauna. All I have is a
>Coke.

THE WOMEN:
In a club! In a night club!

GERMAINE:
God only knows what she does there.

ROSE:
Maybe she tries to get picked up.

ANGELINE:
But I tell you, I don't do anything wrong!

PIERRETTE:
It's true. She doesn't do anything wrong.

ROSE, GERMAINE
AND GABRIELLE:
Shut up, you devil. Shut up!

RHEAUNA:
You're no longer my friend, Angéline. I don't know
you.

ANGELINE:
Listen to me, Rhéauna, you must listen! I can
explain everything if you'll only let me . . .

ROSE, GERMAINE
AND GABRIELLE:
A club! The fastest road to hell!

ALL THE WOMEN: *except the girls*
The road to hell, the road to hell! If you go there,
you'll lose your soul! Cursed drinking, cursed
dancing! That's the kind of place where our men go
wrong and spend their money on women of sin!

ROSE, GERMAINE
AND GABRIELLE:
Women of sin like you, Pierrette!

ALL THE WOMEN: *except the girls*
>Shame on you, Angéline Sauvé, to spend your time in this sinful way!

RHEAUNA:
>But Angéline, a club! It's worse than hell!

PIERRETTE: *laughing heartily*
>If hell is anything like the club I work at, I wouldn't mind an eternity there!

ROSE, GERMAINE
AND GABRIELLE:
>Shut up, Pierrette. The devil has your tongue!

LINDA,
GINETTE AND LISE:
>The devil? Come on! Get with the times! The clubs are not the end of the world! They're no worse than any place else. They're fun! They're lots of fun. The clubs are lots of fun.

THE WOMEN:
>Ah! Youth is blind! Youth is blind! You're gonna lose yourselves, you foolish girls. You're gonna lose yourselves and then you'll come crying to us. But it'll be too late! It'll be too late! Watch out! You be careful of these cursed places! We don't always know it when we fall, but when we get back up, it's too late!

LISE:
>Too late! It's too late! Oh my God, it's too late!

GERMAINE:
>I hope at least you'll go to confession, Angéline Sauvé!

ROSE:

And to think that every Sunday I see you at Communion . . . Communion with a sin like that on your conscience!

GABRIELLE:

A mortal sin!

**ROSE, GERMAINE
AND GABRIELLE:**

How many times have we been told . . . It's a mortal sin to set foot in a club!

ANGELINE:

That's enough. Shut up and listen to me!

THE WOMEN:

Never! You've no excuse!

ANGELINE:

Rhéauna, will you listen to me! We're old friends. We've been together for thirty-five years. You mean a lot to me, but there are times when I want to see other people. You know how I am. I like to have fun. Clubs aren't all bad, you know. I've been going for four years and I never did a thing that made me ashamed. And the people who work there, they're no worse than us. I want to meet new people, Rhéauna! Rhéauna, I've never laughed in my life!

RHEAUNA:

There are better places to laugh. Angéline, you're going to lose your soul. Tell me you won't go back.

ANGELINE:

Listen, Rhéauna, I can't! I like to go there, don't you understand. I like it!

RHEAUNA:

You must promise or I'll never speak to you again.
It's up to you. It's me or the club. If you only knew
how that hurts, my best friend sneaking off to a
night club. How do you think that looks, Angéline?
What will people say when they see you going there?
Especially that place where Pierrette works. It's the
lowest of them all! You must never go back, Angéline, you hear? If you do, it's finished between us.
Finished! You ought to be ashamed!

ANGELINE:

Rhéauna, you can't ask me not to go back . . .
Rhéauna, answer me!

RHEAUNA:

Until you promise, not another word!

> *The lights come up. ANGELINE sits in a
> corner. PIERRETTE joins her.*

ANGELINE:

Why did you have to come here tonight?

PIERRETTE:

Let them talk. They love to get hysterical. They know
damn well you don't do anything wrong at the club.
In five minutes, they'll have forgotten about it.

ANGELINE:

You think so, eh? Well, what about Rhéauna? You
think she'll forgive me just like that? And Mme. de
Courval who's in charge of recreation for the parish,
also President of the Altar Society at Our Lady of
Perpetual Help! You think she'll continue speaking
to me? And your sisters who can't stand you
because you work in a club! I'm telling you it's
hopeless!

GERMAINE:
Pierrette!

PIERRETTE:
Listen, Germaine, Angéline feels bad enough. So let's not fight, eh? I came here to see you and to paste stamps, so that's what I'm gonna do. And I don't have the plague, okay? Just leave us alone. Don't worry. The two of us'll stay out of your way. After tonight, if you want, I won't come back anymore... But I can't leave Angéline by herself.

ANGELINE:
You can go if you want, Pierrette...

PIERRETTE:
No, I want to stay.

ANGELINE:
Okay, then I'll go.

LISETTE:
Why don't they both leave!

ANGELINE gets up.

ANGELINE: *to RHEAUNA*
Are you coming?

RHEAUNA doesn't answer.

Okay. I'll leave the door unlocked...

She goes toward the door. The lights go out. Spotlight on ANGELINE SAUVE.

It's easy to judge people. It's easy to judge them, but you have to look at both sides of the coin. The people I've met in that club are my best friends. No

one has ever treated me so well . . . Not even Rhéauna.
I have fun with those people. I can laugh with them.
I was brought up by nuns in the parish halls who did
the best they could, poor souls, but knew nothing. I
was fifty-five years old when I learned to laugh. And
it was only by chance. Because Pierrette took me to
her club one night. Oh, I didn't want to go. She had
to drag me there. But, you know, the minute I got
in the door, I knew what it was to go through life
without having any fun. I suppose clubs aren't for
everyone, but me, I like them. And of course, it's not
true that I only have a Coke. Of course, I drink liquor!
I don't have much but still, it makes me happy. I
don't do anyone any harm and I buy myself two
hours of pleasure every week. But this was bound to
happen someday. I knew I'd get caught sooner or
later. I knew it. What am I going to do now? Dear
God, what am I going to do? *Pause.* Damn it all!
Everyone deserves to get some fun out of life!
Pause. I always said that if I got caught I'd stop
going . . . But I don't know if I can . . . And Rhéauna
will never go along with that. *Pause.* Ah, well, I
suppose Rhéauna is worth more than Pierrette. *She
gives a long sigh.* I guess the party's over . . .

>   *She goes off. Lights out.*

>   *Spotlight on YVETTE LONGPRE.*

YVETTE:
Last week, my sister-in-law, Fleur-Ange, had a
birthday. They had a real nice party for her. There
was a whole gang of us there. First there was her and
her family, eh? Oscar David, her husband, Fleur-
Ange David, that's her, and their seven kids:
Raymonde, Claude, Lisette, Fernand, Réal, Micheline
and Yves. Her husband's parents, Aurèle David and
his wife, Ozéla David, were there too. Next, there was
my sister-in-law's mother, Blanche Tremblay. Her

father wasn't there 'cause he's dead . . . Then there were the other guests: Antonio Fournier, his wife, Rita, Germaine Gervais, also, Wilfred Gervais, Armand Gervais, George-Albert Gervais, Louis Thibault, Rose Campeau, Daniel Lemoyne and his wife, Rose-Aimée, Roger Joly, Hormidas Guay, Simmone Laflamme, Napoléon Gauvin, Anne-Marie Turgeon, Conrad Joanette, Léa Liasse, Jeanette Landreville, Nina Laplante, Robertine Portelance, Gilberte Morrissette, Laura Cadieux, Rodolphe Quintal, Willie Sanregret, Lilianne Beaupré, Virginie Latour, Alexandre Thibodeau, Ovila Gariépy, Roméo Bacon and his wife, Juliette, Mimi Bleau, Pit Cadieux, Ludger Champagne, Rosaire Rouleau, Roger Chabot, Antonio Simard, Alexandrine Smith, Philémon Langlois, Eliane Meunier, Marcel Morel, Grégoire Cinq-Mars, Théodore Fortier, Hermine Héroux and us, my husband, Euclide, and me. And I think that's just about everyone . . .

The lights come back up.

GERMAINE:
Okay, now let's get back to work, eh?

ROSE:
On your toes, girls. Let's go!

DES-NEIGES:
We're not doing badly, are we? Look at all I've pasted . . .

MARIE-ANGE:
What about all you've stolen . . .

LISETTE:
You want to hand me more stamps, Mme. Lauzon . . .

GERMAINE:

Sure . . . Coming right up . . . Here's a whole bunch.

RHEAUNA:

Angéline! Angéline! It can't be true!

LINDA: *to PIERRETTE*

Hello, Pierrette.

PIERRETTE:

Hi! How're you doing?

LINDA:

Oh, not too good. Ma and I are always fighting and I'm really getting sick of it. She's always bitching about nothing, you know? I'd sure like to get out of here.

GERMAINE:

The retreats will be starting pretty soon, eh?

ROSE:

Yeah! That's what they said last Sunday.

MARIE-ANGE:

I hope we won't be getting the same priest as last year . . .

GERMAINE:

Me too! I didn't like him either. What a bore.

PIERRETTE:

Well, what's stopping you? You could come and stay with me . . .

LINDA:

Are you kidding? They'd disown me on the spot!

LISETTE:

No, we've got a new one coming this year.

DES-NEIGES:

Oh yeah? Who's it gonna be?

LISETTE:

A certain Abbé Rochon. They say he's excellent. I was talking to l'Abbé Gagné the other day and he tells me he's one of his best friends . . .

ROSE: *to GABRIELLE*

There she goes again with her Abbé Gagné. We'll be hearing about him all night! You'd think she was in love with him. Abbé Gagné this, Abbé Gagné that . . . Well, as far as I'm concerned, he's a pain in the ass . . .

GABRIELLE:

I agree. He's too modern for me. It's okay to take care of parish activities, but he shouldn't forget he's a priest! A man of God!

LISETTE:

Oh, but the man is a saint . . . You should get to know him, Mme. Dubuc. I'm sure you'd like him . . . When he's talking, you'd swear it was the Lord himself addressing you.

THERESE:

Don't exaggerate . . .

LISETTE:

And the children! They adore him. Oh, that reminds me, the children in the parish are organizing a variety night for next month. I hope you can all make it because it should be very impressive. They've been working on it for ages . . .

DES-NEIGES:

    What's on the programme?

LISETTE:

    Well, it's quite interesting. They're going to have a whole lot of numbers. Mme. Gladu's little boy is going to sing . . .

ROSE:

    Not again! I'm getting sick of that kid. You know, every since he went on television, his mother's had her nose in the air. She thinks she's a real star!

LISETTE:

    But the child has a lovely voice.

ROSE:

    Oh yeah? Well, he looks like a girl with his mouth all puckered up like a turkey's ass.

GABRIELLE:

    Rose!

LISETTE:

    Diane Aubin will give a demonstration of aquatic swimming at the city pool. That's where it's all taking place, you know. It should be a stunning display . . .

ROSE:

    Any door prizes?

LISETTE:

    Oh yes, lots. And the final event of the evening will be a giant bingo.

THE OTHER
WOMEN: *except the girls*

    A bingo!

      Blackout.

*When the lights come back up, the women are
all at the edge of the stage.*

LISETTE:
Ode to Bingo!

*While ROSE, GERMAINE, GABRIELLE,
THERESE and MARIE-ANGE recite the Ode
to Bingo, the four other women call out bingo
numbers in counterpoint.*

ROSE, GERMAINE, GABRIELLE,
THERESE AND MARIE-ANGE:
Me, there's nothing in the world that I like more than
bingo. You know, we orgainize one in the parish al-
most every month. I get ready two days in advance.
I'm a nervous wreck. I can't sit still. I can't even
think about anything else. When the big day arrives,
I'm so excited I can't do a bit of work around the
house. But the minute supper's over, I put on my
Sunday best and not even a freight train would keep
me out of the lady's house where we're going to play.
I love playing bingo! I adore playing bingo! There's
nothing in the world that I like more than bingo!
As soon as we arrive, we get rid of our coats and head
straight for the room where we're going to play.
Sometimes it's the living room the lady has cleared,
sometimes it's the kitchen and there's even times
when we use the bedroom. We sit down at the tables,
hand out the cards, set up the chips and the game
begins!

*The women who are calling the numbers
continue alone for a moment.*

I'm telling you, I get so excited I go right off my
rocker. I'm all mixed up. I sweat like a pig. I screw
up the numbers. I put my chips in the wrong squares.
I make the caller repeat the numbers. Oh, I get into

a terrible state! I love playing bingo! I adore playing
bingo! There's nothing in the world that I like more
than bingo! The game's almost over! I've got three
more tries. Two on top and one across! I need the
B-14! Give me the B-14! The B-14! The B-14! I
look at the others . . . Shit, they've got as much
chance as me. What am I gonna do? I've gotta win!
I've gotta win! I've gotta win!

LISETTE:
> B-14!

THE OTHERS:
> Bingo! Bingo! I've won! I knew it! I knew I
> couldn't lose! I've won! Hey, what did I win?

LISETTE:
> Last month we had Chinese dog door stops. But
> this month, this month, we've got ashtray floor
> lamps!

THE OTHERS:
> I love playing bingo! I adore playing bingo! There's
> nothing in the world that I like more than bingo!
> What a shame they don't have 'em more often. The
> more they have, the happier it makes me! Long live
> the Chinese dogs! Long live the ashtray floor lamps!
> Long live bingo!

ROSE:
> I'm getting thirsty.

GERMAINE:
> Oh God, I forgot the drinks! Linda, get out the
> Cokes.

OLIVINE:
> Coke . . . Coke . . . Yeah . . . Yeah, Coke . . .

THERESE:

> Take it easy, Mme. Dubuc. You'll get a Coke like everyone else. But drink it properly! No spilling it like last time.

ROSE:

> She's driving me up the wall with her mother-in-law . . .

GABRIELLE:

> Forget it, Rose. There's been enough fighting already.

GERMAINE:

> Yeah! Just keep quiet and paste. You're not doing a thing!

> *Spotlight on the refrigerator. The following scene takes place by the refrigerator door.*

LISE: *to LINDA*

> I've got to talk to you, Linda . . .

LINDA:

> I know, you told me at the restaurant . . . But it's hardly a good time . . .

LISE:

> It won't take long and I've got to tell somebody. I can't hide it much longer. I'm too upset. And Linda, you're my best friend . . . Linda, I'm going to have a baby.

LINDA:

> What! But that's crazy! Are you sure?

LISE:

> Yes, I'm sure. The doctor told me.

LINDA:
>What are you gonna do?

LISE:
>I don't know. I'm so depressed! I haven't told my parents yet. My father'll kill me. I know he will. When the doctor told me, I felt like jumping off the balcony . . .

PIERRETTE:
>Listen, Lise . . .

LINDA:
>Did you hear?

PIERRETTE:
>Yeah! I know you're in a jam, kid, but . . . I might be able to help you . . .

LISE:
>Yeah? How?

PIERRETTE:
>Well, I know a doctor . . .

LINDA:
>Pierrette, she can't do that!

PIERRETTE:
>Come on, it's not dangerous . . . He does it twice a week, this guy.

LISE:
>I've thought about it already, Linda . . . But I didn't know anyone . . . And I'm scared to try it alone.

PIERRETTE:
>Don't ever do that! It's too dangerous! But with this doctor . . . I can arrange it, if you like. A week from now you'll be all fixed up.

LINDA:

Lise, that's not what you want! It's a crime!

LISE:

What else can I do? It's the only way out. I don't
want the thing to be born. Look what happened to
Manon Belair. She was in the same boat and now
her life's all screwed up because she's got that kid on
her hands.

LINDA:

What about the father? Can't he marry you?

LISE:

Are you kidding! I don't even know where he is.
He just took off somewhere. Sure, he promised me
a lot. We were gonna be happy. He was making all this
money. I thought everything was roses. Presents here,
presents there. No end to it. It was really nice for a
while . . . But shit, I knew this would happen. I just
knew it. Why do I always wind up in the shit when
all I want to do is get out of it? Christ, I'm sick of
working at Kresge's. I want to make something of my
life. I want to get somewhere. I want a car, a decent
place to live, some nice clothes. I've got nothing to
wear but my uniform, for Chrissake! I've never had
any money. I've always had to scrounge for it . . .
But I want things to change! I want things to get
better. I don't want to be cheap anymore. I came
in the backdoor, but goddamn it, I'm gonna go out
the front! And nothing's gonna get in my way, you
hear. Nothing's gonna stop me! You watch, Linda.
You just watch. In two or three years, you're gonna
see that Lise Paquette is a somebody! And money,
she's gonna have it, okay?

LINDA:

You're off to a bad start.

LISE:

That's just it! I've made a mistake and I want to
correct it. After this, I can make a fresh start. You
understand, don't you, Pierrette?

PIERRETTE:

Sure, I do. I know what it is to want to be rich. Look
at me. When I was your age, I left home because I
wanted to make some money. But I didn't start by
working in a dime store. Oh, no! I went straight to
the club. Because that's where the money was. And
it won't be long now before I'm rolling in it. Johnny
told me . . .

ROSE, GERMAINE
AND GABRIELLE:

Goddamn Johnny! Goddamn Johnny!

GINETTE:

What's going on over here?

LISE:

Nothing, nothing. *To PIERRETTE.* We'll talk
about it later . . .

GINETTE:

Talk about what?

LISE:

Forget it. It's nothing!

GINETTE:

Can't you tell me?

LISE:

Leave me alone, will you?

PIERRETTE:

Come on, we can talk over here . . .

GERMAINE:

    What's happening to those Cokes?

LINDA:

    Coming, coming . . .

    The lights come back up.

GABRIELLE:

    Hey, Rose, you know that blue suit of yours? How much did you pay for it?

ROSE:

    Which one?

GABRIELLE:

    You know, the one with the white lace around the collar?

ROSE:

    Oh, that one . . . I got it for $9.98.

GABRIELLE:

    That's what I thought. Imagine, today I saw the same one at Reitmans for $14.98 . . .

ROSE:

    No kidding! I told you I got it cheap, eh?

LISETTE:

    My sister Micheline just found a new job. She's started to work with F.B.I. machines.

MARIE-ANGE:

    Oh yeah! I hear those things are tough on the nerves. The girls who work them have to change jobs every six months. My sister-in-law, Simonne's daughter, had a nervous breakdown over one. Simonne just phoned to tell me about it . . .

ROSE:

Oh my God, I just remembered, Linda. You're
wanted on the phone!

LINDA runs to the phone.

LINDA:

Hello, Robert? How long have you been waiting?

GINETTE:

Tell me.

LISE:

No. Beat it, will you? I want to talk to Pierrette . . .
Go on, get lost!

GINETTE:

Okay, I hear you! You're happy to have me around
when there's nobody else, eh? But when someone
more interesting comes along . . .

LINDA:

Listen, Robert, it's not my fault! I just found out!

THERESE:

Here, Mme. Dubuc, hide these!

ROSE:

How are things at your place, Ginette?

GINETTE:

Oh, same as usual, I guess . . . Lots of fights . . .
Nothing new. My mother still drinks . . . And my dad
gets mad . . . And they go on fighting . . .

ROSE:

Poor kid . . . And your sister?

GINETTE:

Suzanne? Oh, she's still the brainy one. She can't do anything wrong, you know. "Now there's a girl who uses her head. You should be more like her, Ginette. She's making something of her life." . . . Nobody else even counts, especially me. But they always did like her best. And, of course, now that she's a school teacher, you'd think she was a saint or something.

ROSE:

Now, Ginette. Aren't you exaggerating a bit?

GINETTE:

No, I'm serious . . . My mother's never cared about me. It's always, "Suzanne's the prettiest. Suzanne's the nicest." . . . Every goddamned day, till I'm sick of hearing it! Even Lise doesn't like me anymore!

LINDA: *on the phone*

Oh, go to hell! If you don't want to listen, why should I talk? Phone me back when you're in a better mood!

She hangs up.

For Chrissake, Aunt Rose, why didn't you tell me I was wanted on the phone? Now he's pissed off at me!

ROSE:

Isn't she polite! You see how polite she is?

Spotlight on PIERRETTE.

PIERRETTE:

When I left home, I was head over heels in love. I couldn't even see straight. Nothing existed for me but Johnny. Johnny, the bastard who made me waste ten years of my life. Here I am thirty years old and I feel like sixty. The things that guy got me to do! And me, the idiot. I listened to him. Ten years I worked his club for him. I was good-looking. I brought in the customers and that was fine as long as it lasted . . . But now . . . Now I've had it. I'm fucked. I feel like jumping off a goddamn bridge. All I got left is the bottle. And that's what I've been doing since Friday. Poor Lise, she thinks she's done for just because she's pregnant. She's still young. I'm gonna give her my doctor's name . . . He'll fix her up. It'll be easy for her to start over. Not me though. I'm too old. A girl who's been at it for ten years is all washed up. Finished. And how am I gonna explain that to my sisters? They'll never understand. I don't know what I'm gonna do now. I just don't know.

LISE:

I don't know what I'm gonna do now. I just don't know. It's a serious thing, an abortion. I've heard enough stories to know that. But I guess I'm better off going to see Pierrette's doctor than trying to do it myself. Ah, why do these things always happen to me? Pierrette, she's lucky. Working in the same club for ten years. Making lots of money . . . And she's in love too! I wouldn't mind being in her shoes. Even if her family can't stand her at least she's happy on her own.

PIERRETTE:

He dropped me, just like that! "It's all over," he said. I don't need you anymore. You're too old and too ugly. So pack your bags and beat it. That son-of-a-bitch! He didn't leave me a nickle! Not a goddamn nickle! After all I did for him. Ten years! Ten years for nothing. That's enough to make you want to pack it in. What am I gonna do now, eh? What? Be a two-bit waitress at Kresge's like Lise? No thanks! Kresge's is fine for kids and old ladies, but not for me. I don't know what I'm gonna do. I just don't

96

know. It's hell pretending everything's great. But I
can't tell Linda and Lise I'm finished. *Silence.*
Yeah . . . I guess there's nothing left but booze . . .
Good thing I like that . . .

LISE: *interspersed throughout PIERRETTE's last speech*
I'm scared! Dear God, I'm scared!

She approaches PIERRETTE.

Are you sure this is gonna work, Pierrette? I'm so
frightened!

PIERRETTE: *laughing*
Sure, sure. Everything will work out fine. You'll see.
You'll be okay . . .

The lights come back up.

MARIE-ANGE:
It's not even safe to go to a show, you know. Like
I went to the Rex the other day to see Belmondo
in something. I forget what. My husband stayed
home. Well, all of a sudden, right in the middle of
the show, this smelly old bum sat down next to me
and started fiddling with my knee. Now, I was
embarrassed, but I wasn't at a loss, if you know what
I mean. So I stood up, took my purse and smashed
him right in his ugly face.

DES-NEIGES:
Good for you, Mme. Brouillette! I always carry a
hat pin when I go to the show. You never know
what'll happen. And the first one who tries to get
fresh with me . . . But I've never used it yet.

ROSE:
Hey, Germaine, these Cokes are pretty warm.

GERMAINE:

When are you gonna stop criticizing, eh? When?

LISE:

Linda, you got a pencil and paper?

LINDA:

I'm telling you, Lise, don't do it!

LISE:

I know what I'm doing. I've made up my mind and nothing's gonna make me change it.

RHEAUNA: *to THERESE*

What are you doing there?

THERESE:

Shh! Not so loud! You should take some too. A few books, no one's gonna know.

RHEAUNA:

I'm no thief!

THERESE:

It's not a question of stealing, Mlle. Bibeau. She got them for nothing and there's a million of 'em. A million!

RHEAUNA:

That has nothing to do with it. She invited us here to paste her stamps and we've got no right to steal them!

GERMAINE: *to ROSE*

What are those two talking about? I don't like all this whispering . . .

She goes over to RHEAUNA and THERESE.

THERESE: *seeing her coming*
Oh... Yeah... You add two cups of water and stir.

RHEAUNA:
What? *Noticing GERMAINE.* Oh! Yes! She was giving me a recipe.

GERMAINE:
A recipe for what?

RHEAUNA:
Doughnuts!

THERESE:
Chocolate pudding!

GERMAINE:
Well, which is it? Doughnuts or chocolate pudding?

She comes back to ROSE.

Listen, Rose, there's something fishy going on around here.

ROSE: *who has just hidden a few books in her purse*
Don't be silly... You're imagining things...

GERMAINE:
And I think Linda's spending too much time with Pierrette. Linda, come here!

LINDA:
Just a minute, Ma...

GERMAINE:
I said come here! That means now. Not tomorrow!

LINDA:

Okay! Don't get so excited ... Yeah, what is it?

GABRIELLE:

Stay with us for a bit ... You've been with your aunt long enough.

LINDA:

So? What's wrong with that?

GERMAINE:

What's going on between her and Lise there?

LINDA:

Oh ... Nothing ...

GERMAINE:

Answer when you're spoken to!

ROSE:

Lise wrote something down a while ago.

LINDA:

It was just an address ...

GERMAINE:

Not Pierrette's, I hope! If I ever find out you've been to her place, you're gonna hear from me, understand?

LINDA:

Will you lay off! I'm old enough to know what I'm doing!

She goes back to PIERRETTE.

ROSE:

Maybe it's none of my business, Germaine, but ...

GERMAINE:
>   Why, what's the matter now?

ROSE:
>   Your Linda's picking up some pretty bad habits . . .

GERMAINE:
>   You can say that again! But don't worry, Rose. I
>   can handle her. She's gonna straighten out fast. And
>   as for Pierrette, that's the last time she'll set foot
>   in this house. I'll throw her down the goddamn
>   stairs!

MARIE-ANGE:
>   Have you noticed Mme. Bergeron's daughter lately?
>   Wouldn't you say she's been putting on weight?

LISETTE:
>   Yes, I did notice that . . .

THERESE: *insinuating*
>   Strange, isn't it? It's all in her middle.

ROSE:
>   I guess the sap's running a bit early this year.

MARIE-ANGE:
>   She tries to hide it too. It's beginning to show
>   though.

THERESE:
>   And how! I wonder who could have done it?

LISETTE:
>   It's probably her step-father . . .

GERMAINE:
>   Wouldn't surprise me in the least. He's been after
>   her ever since he married her mother.

THERESE:

It must be awful in that house. I feel sorry for
Monique. She's so young . . .

ROSE:

Maybe so, but she knows what it's all about. Just
look at the way she dresses. Why, last summer, I was
embarrassed to look at her! And you know me. I'm
no prude. Remember those red shorts she was
wearing? Those short shorts? Well, I said it then,
and I'll say it again, "Monique Bergeron is gonna turn
out bad. She's got the devil in her, that girl, a real
demon. Besides, she's a redhead." . . . No, you can
say what you like, those unwed mothers deserve
what they get and I got no sympathy for 'em.

LISE starts to get up.

PIERRETTE:

Take it easy, kid!

ROSE:

It's true! It's their own damn fault! I'm not talking
about the ones who get raped. That's different. But
an ordinary girl who gets herself pregnant, uh uh . . .
She gets no sympathy from me. It's too goodamn
bad! I tell you, if my Carmen ever came home
knocked up, she'd go sailing right through the
window! Not that I'm worried about her, mind you.
She'd never do something like that . . . Nope, for me
unwed mothers are all the same. A bunch of depraved
sluts. You know what my husband calls 'em, eh?
Cockteasers!

LISE:

I'll kill her if she doesn't shut up!

GINETTE:

What for? If you ask me, she's right.

LISE:
>   Why don't you just fuck off!

PIERRETTE:
>   That's a bit much, isn't it, Rose?

ROSE:
>   Listen, Pierrette, we know you're an expert on these
>   matters. We know you can't be shocked. Maybe you
>   think it's normal, but we don't. The only way to
>   prevent it . . .

PIERRETTE: *laughing*
>   I know lots of ways. Ever heard of the pill?

ROSE:
>   It's no use talking to you! That's not what I meant!
>   I'm against free love! I'm a Catholic! So leave us
>   alone and stay where you belong, you filthy pig!

LISETTE:
>   I think perhaps you exaggerate, Mme. Ouimet. There
>   are occasions when girls can get themselves in trouble
>   and it's not entirely their fault.

ROSE:
>   You! You believe everything they tell you in those
>   stupid French movies!

LISETTE:
>   What have you got against French movies?

ROSE:
>   Nothing. I like English ones better, that's all.
>   French movies, they're too realistic, too far-fetched.
>   You shouldn't believe what they say. They always
>   make you feel sorry for the girl who gets pregnant.
>   It's never anyone else's fault. Well, do you feel sorry
>   for tramps like that? I don't! A movie's a movie
>   and life's life!

LISE:

I'll murder the stupid bitch! Goddamn pig! She goes around judging everyone and she's got no more brains than a . . . And as for her Carmen. Well, I happen to know her Carmen and believe me, she does a lot more than tease! She oughtta clean up her own house before she shits on everyone else's.

Spotlight on ROSE OUIMET.

ROSE:

That's right. Life is life and no goddamn French-man ever made a movie about that! Sure, any old actress can make you feel sorry for her in a movie. Easy as pie! And when she's finished work, she can go home to her big fat mansion and climb into her big fat bed that's twice the size of my bedroom, for Chrissake! But the rest of us, when we get up in the morning . . . *Silence.* When I wake up in the morning, he's lying there staring at me . . . Waiting. Every morning, I open my eyes and there he is, waiting! Every night, I get into bed and there he is, waiting! He's always there, always after me, always hanging over me like a vulture. Goddamn sex! It's never that way in the movies, is it? Oh no, in the movies it's always fun! Besides, who cares about a woman who's gotta spend her life with a pig just 'cause she said yes to him once? Well, I'm telling you, no fucking movie was ever this sad. Because a movie don't last a lifetime! *Silence.* Why did I ever do it? Why? I should have said no. I should have yelled it at the top of my lungs and been an old maid instead. At least I'd have had some peace. I was so ignorant in those days. Christ, I didn't know what I was in for. All I could think of was "the Holy State of Matrimony!" You gotta be stupid to bring up your kids like that, knowing nothing. You gotta be so stupid! I tell you one thing. My Carmen won't get caught like that. Because me, I've been telling her for years what men are really worth. She won't be able to say I didn't warn her! *On the verge of tears.* She won't end up like me, forty-four years old, with a two year old kid and another one on the way, with a stupid slob of a husband who can't understand a thing, who demands his "rights" at least twice a day, three hundred and sixty-five days of the year. When you get to be forty and you realize you've got nothing behind you and nothing in front of you, it makes you want to dump the whole thing and start all over. But a woman can't do that . . . A woman gets grabbed by the throat and she's gotta stay that way right to the end!

The lights come back up.

GABRIELLE:
Well, I happen to like French movies, especially the sad ones. They always make me cry. They're so beautiful. And those Frenchmen. They're much better looking than Canadians. They're real men!

GERMAINE:
Now just a minute! That's not true.

MARIE-ANGE:
Come on! The little peckers don't even come up to my shoulder. And they act like girls! Of course, what do you expect? They're all queer!

GABRIELLE:
I beg your pardon. Some of them are men! And I don't mean like our husbands.

MARIE-ANGE:
Compared to our husbands anything looks good.

LISETTE:
You don't mix serviettes with paper napkins.

GERMAINE:
Okay, so our husbands are rough, but our actors are just as good and just as good-looking as any one of those French actors from France.

GABRIELLE:
Well, I wouldn't say no to Jean Marais. Now there's a *real* man!

OLIVINE:
Coke ... Coke ... More ... Coke ...

THERESE:
Be quiet, Mme. Dubuc!

OLIVINE:
Coke! Coke!

ROSE:
Hey, can't you shut her up? It's impossible to work! Shove a Coke in her mouth, Germaine. That'll keep her quiet.

GERMAINE:
I don't know if I got anymore.

ROSE:
Jesus, you didn't buy much, did you? You're really pinching the pennies.

RHEAUNA: *as she steals some stamps*
Oh, what the heck. Three more books and I can get my chrome dustpan.

ANGELINE comes in.

ANGELINE:
Hello ... *To RHEAUNA.* I came back ...

THE OTHERS: *coldly*
Hello . . .

ANGELINE:
I went to see l'Abbé Castelneau . . .

PIERRETTE:
She didn't even look at me!

MARIE-ANGE:
What does she want with Mlle. Bibeau?

DES-NEIGES:
I think to ask forgiveness. You know, after all is said and done, she's really a good person and she knows what she ought to do. It'll all work out for the best, you'll see.

GERMAINE:
While we're waiting, I'm gonna see how many books we've filled.

The women sit up in their chairs.

GABRIELLE hesitates, then speaks.

GABRIELLE:
Oh, Germaine, I forgot to tell you. I found a corset-maker. Her name's Angélina Giroux. Come over here, I'll tell you about her.

RHEAUNA:
I knew you'd come back to me, Angéline. I'm very happy. You'll see, we'll pray together and the Good Lord will forget all about it. God's not stupid, you know.

LISE:
> Well, Pierrette, it looks like they're friends again.

PIERRETTE:
> I'll be goddamned!

ANGELINE:
> I'll just say goodbye to Pierrette and explain . . .

RHEAUNA:
> No, you'd best not say another word to her. Stay
> with me and leave her alone. That chapter's closed.

ANGELINE:
> Whatever you say.

PIERRETTE:
> Well, that's that. The old bitch has won. I guess there's
> nothing more for me to do, so I might as well leave.

GERMAINE:
> Gaby, you're terrific. I'd almost given up hope. It's
> not everyone can make me a corset. I'll go see her
> next week.

>> *She goes over to the box that is supposed to hold
>> the completed books. The women follow her with
>> their eyes.*

> My God, there isn't much here! Where are all the
> booklets? There's no more than a dozen in the box.
> Maybe they're . . . No, the table's empty!

>> *Silence.*

>> *GERMAINE looks at all the women.*

> What's going on around here?

THE OTHERS:
Well... Ah... I don't know... Really...

> *They pretend to search for the books.*
> *GERMAINE stations herself in front of the*
> *door.*

GERMAINE:
Where are my stamps?

ROSE:
Come on, Germaine. Let's look for them.

GERMAINE:
They're not in the box and they're not on the table.
I want to know what's happened to my stamps!

OLIVINE: *pulling stamps out from under her clothes*
Stamps? Stamps... Stamps...

> *She laughs.*

THERESE:
Mme. Dubuc, hide that... Goddamn it, Mme.
Dubuc!

MARIE-ANGE:
Dear Ste-Anne!

DES-NEIGES:
Pray for us!

GERMAINE:
But her clothes are full of them! What the ...
She's got them everywhere! Here.... And here...
Thérèse... Don't tell me it's you.

THERESE:
Good heavens, no! I swear, I had no idea!

GERMAINE:

Let me see your purse.

THERESE:

Germaine, if that's all the faith you have in me . . .

ROSE:

Germaine, don't be ridiculous!

GERMAINE:

You too, Rose. I want to see your purse. I want to see all your purses. Every one of them!

DES-NEIGES:

I refuse! I've never been so insulted!

YVETTE:

Me neither.

LISETTE:

I'll never set foot in here again!

GERMAINE grabs THERESE's bag and opens it. She pulls out several books.

GERMAINE:

Ahah! I knew it! I bet it's the same with all of you! You bastards!! You won't get out of here alive! I'll knock the daylights out of every one of you!

PIERRETTE:

I'll help you, Germaine. Nothing but a pack of thieves! And they look down their noses at me!

GERMAINE:

Show me your purses.

She grabs ROSE's purse.

Look at that . . . And that!

She grabs another purse.

More here. And look, still more! You too, Mlle. Bibeau? There's only three, but even so!

ANGELINE:
Oh, Rhéauna, you too!

GERMAINE:
All of you, thieves! The whole bunch of you, you hear me? Thieves!

MARIE-ANGE:
You don't deserve all those stamps.

DES-NEIGES:
Yeah, why you more than anyone else?

ROSE:
You've made us feel like shit with your million stamps!

GERMAINE:
But those stamps are mine!

LISETTE:
They ought to be for everyone!

THE OTHERS:
Yeah, everyone!

GERMAINE:
But they're mine! Give them back to me!

THE OTHERS:
Never!

MARIE-ANGE:
There's still lots more in the boxes. Let's help ourselves.

DES-NEIGES:
>Good idea.

YVETTE:
>I'm gonna fill up my purse.

GERMAINE:
>Stop! Keep your hands off!

THERESE:
>Here, Mme. Dubuc, take these! Here's some more.

MARIE-ANGE:
>Come here, Mlle. Verrette. There's tons of them.
>Give me a hand.

PIERRETTE:
>Get your hands out of there!

GERMAINE:
>My stamps! My stamps!

ROSE:
>Help me, Gaby, I took too many!

GERMAINE:
>My stamps! My stamps!

>*A huge battle follows. The women steal all the stamps they can. PIERRETTE and GERMAINE try to stop them. LINDA and LISE stay seated in the corner and watch without moving. Screams are heard as some of the women begin fighting.*

MARIE-ANGE:
>Give me those, they're mine!

ROSE:
    That's a lie, they're mine!

LISETTE: *to GABY*
    Will you let go of me! Let me go!

> *They start throwing stamps and books at one*
> *another. Everybody grabs all they can get their*
> *hands on, throwing stamps everywhere, out the*
> *door, even out the window. OLIVINE DUBUC*
> *starts cruising around in her wheelchair singing*
> *"O Canada." A few women go out with their*
> *loot of stamps. ROSE and GABRIELLE stay a*
> *bit longer than the others.*

GERMAINE:
    My sisters! My own sisters!

> *GABRIELLE and ROSE go out. The only ones*
> *left in the kitchen are GERMAINE, LINDA*
> *and PIERRETTE. GERMAINE collapses into*
> *a chair.*

My stamps! My stamps!

> *PIERRETTE puts her arms around GERMAINE's*
> *shoulders.*

PIERRETTE:
    Don't cry, Germaine.

GERMAINE:
    Don't talk to me. Get out! You're no better than
    the rest of them!

PIERRETTE:
    But . . .

GERMAINE:

Get out! I never want to see you again!

PIERRETTE:

But I tried to help you! I'm on your side, Germaine!

GERMAINE:

Get out and leave me alone! Don't speak to me. I don't want to see anyone!

PIERRETTE goes out slowly. LINDA also heads towards the door.

LINDA:

It'll be some job cleaning all that up!

GERMAINE:

My God! My God! My stamps! There's nothing left! Nothing! Nothing! My beautiful new home! My lovely furniture! Gone! My stamps! My stamps!

She falls to her knees beside the chair, picking up the remaining stamps. She is crying very hard. We hear all the others outside singing "O Canada." As the song continues, GERMAINE regains her courage. She finishes "O Canada" with the others, standing at attention, with tears in her eyes. A rain of stamps falls slowly from the ceiling . . .

TALONBOOKS — PLAYS IN PRINT 1979

Colours in the Dark — James Reaney
The Ecstasy of Rita Joe — George Ryga
Captives of the Faceless Drummer — George Ryga
Crabdance — Beverley Simons
Listen to the Wind — James Reaney
Ashes for Easter & Other Monodramas — David Watmough
Esker Mike & His Wife, Agiluk — Herschel Hardin
Sunrise on Sarah — George Ryga
Walsh — Sharon Pollock
The Factory Lab Anthology — Connie Brissenden, ed.
The Trial of Jean-Baptiste M. — Robert Gurik
Battering Ram — David Freeman
Hosanna — Michel Tremblay
Les Belles Soeurs — Michel Tremblay
API 2967 — Robert Gurik
You're Gonna Be Alright Jamie Boy — David Freeman
Bethune — Rod Langley
Preparing — Beverley Simons
Forever Yours Marie-Lou — Michel Tremblay
En Pièces Détachées — Michel Tremblay
Lulu Street — Ann Henry
Three Plays by Eric Nicol — Eric Nicol
Fifteen Miles of Broken Glass — Tom Hendry
Bonjour, là, Bonjour — Michel Tremblay
Jacob's Wake — Michael Cook
On the Job — David Fennario
Sqrieux-de-Dieu — Betty Lambert
Some Angry Summer Songs — John Herbert
The Execution — Marie-Claire Blais
Tiln & Other Plays — Michael Cook
The Great Wave of Civilization — Herschel Hardin
La Duchesse de Langeais & Other Plays — Michel Tremblay
Have — Julius Hay
Cruel Tears — Ken Mitchell and Humphrey & the Dumptrucks
Ploughmen of the Glacier — George Ryga
Nothing to Lose — David Fennario
Les Canadiens — Rick Salutin
Seven Hours to Sundown — George Ryga
Can You See Me Yet? — Timothy Findley
Two Plays — George Woodcock
Ashes — David Rudkin
Spratt — Joe Wiesenfeld
Walls — Christian Bruyere
Boiler Room Suite — Rex Deverell
In a Lifetime — Roland Lepage
After Abraham — Ron Chudley
Sainte-Marie Among the Hurons — James W. Nichol

The Lionel Touch — George Hulme
Balconville — David Fennario
Angel City, Curse of the Starving Class & Other Plays — Sam Shepard
The Primary English Class — Israel Horovitz
Mackerel — Israel Horovitz

TALONBOOKS — THEATRE FOR THE YOUNG

Raft Baby — Dennis Foon
The Windigo — Dennis Foon
Heracles — Dennis Foon
A Chain of Words — Irene Watts
Apple Butter — James Reaney
Geography Match — James Reaney
Names and Nicknames — James Reaney
Ignoramus — James Reaney
A Teacher's Guide to Theatre for Young People — Jane Baker, ed.
A Mirror of Our Dreams — Joyce Doolittle and Zina Barnieh